A DANGEROUS GIFT

Recent Titles by Emma Stirling from Severn House

A SUMMER ENGAGEMENT
MARRIAGE OF SECRETS
A WOMAN'S TOUCH

A
DANGEROUS GIFT

Emma Stirling

This title first published in Great Britain 1997 by
SEVERN HOUSE PUBLISHERS LTD of
9–15 High Street, Sutton, Surrey SM1 1DF.
Originally published in 1977 in Great Britain under the
Title *Danger in Scarlet* and pseudonym *Elspeth Couper*.
This title first published in the U.S.A. 1998 by
SEVERN HOUSE PUBLISHERS INC of
595 Madison Avenue, New York, N.Y. 10022.

British Library Cataloguing in Publication Data

Stirling, Emma

   A dangerous gift
  1.   Romantic suspense novels
  I.   Title II. Couper, Elspeth.
     Danger in scarlet

  823.9'14 [F]

  ISBN 0 7278 5138 1

Typeset by Palimpsest Book Production Limited,
Polmont, Stirlingshire, Scotland.
Printed and bound in Great Britain by
MPG Books Ltd, Bodmin, Cornwall.

ONE

An air of expectancy hung over Kylie as she opened the door to Paul late that afternoon. They kissed and he looked at her, one eyebrow raised questioningly. 'You are very perky this evening, aren't you?'

'I should be,' Kylie laughed. 'I've just heard the most wonderful news.' She waved the sheet of thick white paper under his nose, her own wrinkling teasingly. 'This is the reason why I can't come with you to Greece this year. I have to go to Africa!'

'Africa!' Paul looked at her in amazement. 'What on earth for? I've never heard anything so foolish . . .'

'Not at all,' she replied solemnly. 'An heiress has her duties and one doesn't inherit an emerald mine every day.'

'An emerald mine! Here, let me see that letter.'

Kylie gave him the letter and watched as he read it. How she loved him, even if, at times, he was a bit wild, unable to settle to anything. A frown appeared between his eyes, and she laughed as he lowered the letter, exclaiming, 'For heaven's sake, Kylie! Your father's mine! Are you really serious about going all that way?'

'How can I *not* be?' she asked, taking the letter back, her eyes scanning the single typed page. 'There *is* no one else.'

Paul stood up. 'But the place is absolutely miles from anywhere! Practically worthless, according to what your mother says.'

'It's not worthless. The mine employs dozens of natives and Daddy and his partner where making a go of it at last. It was more than paying for itself.'

Paul grimaced. 'Humph . . . I don't know about that,

Kylie. From what I gathered from the letters you let me read, the place was practically falling apart. A decrepit old house in the middle of nowhere, the mine shaft probably all decay and jungle rot.'

'The Sheila Mine,' Kylie said defiantly, 'was once a very wealthy proposition.'

Paul hit his forehead with the palm of his hand. 'For heaven's sake!' he repeated, 'don't tell me you believe all that rot? If it was so wealthy why did your father and old Tom Kylie live like hermits in the place, hardly ever emerging into civilization, coming home once in a blue moon . . . ?'

'My father hated civilization, as you call it,' Kylie said, her eyes flashing. 'Even when he *was* able to return to England he never stayed very long. And it wasn't just for the lack of money. He kept mother and I comfortably enough. We could even afford a small car, once I was old enough to drive, and there was that secretarial course for me.'

'Which you're all set to toss away, just like that,' Paul exclaimed, 'just when you've obtained a wonderful position that pays well. Apart from that, there's our engagement! I thought you wanted to plan a spring wedding?'

Kylie drew a deep breath, gazing at him with stricken eyes. 'I do, Paul, I do. I can't just ignore the letter, can I?' she added, weakly.

'You don't have to ignore it, Kylie. Just write to this lawyer chap and tell him to sell the place—at whatever price he can get—and send you the cheque.'

'I can't do that—without ever having seen it . . .'

Paul sighed. 'You're putting me on! Why on earth not? What's so special about a decrepit old mine, way out in the jungle? Miles away from anywhere. It certainly didn't bring either you or your mother happiness, now, did it?'

He gazed at her curiously, seeing the stubborn tilt to

6

the small chin, the gleam in the blue eyes that told him she was deadly serious. She wasn't, he realized, putting him on. Not a bit of it. She meant every word she said. He moved over to the window, gazing across the roof-tops of London to the sparkle that was the Thames, shining silver-grey under a wintry sky.

For a time the noise of the traffic, the grinding of the red buses in the street below, was the only sound. Kylie came up behind him and placing her arms about his waist laid her cheek against his back, feeling the rough tweed of the jacket damp on her skin. It must be raining outside again.

'Don't be cross with me, Paul. I *do* want a spring wedding and you know how much I love you, but my father worked for so long to make this dream come true. To let some stranger take over now . . . Well, I just can't bring myself to think that way, that's all. Say you understand, darling?'

He turned from the window, taking her in his arms. 'I'll say it, but I won't mean it.' His lips touched hers in a kiss and she clung to him, the mine, the letter forgotten for the moment. After a while he pushed her away from him, gazing down into her face with a frown. 'Kylie, baby, the tickets for the cruise are all bought and paid for. The weather promises to be perfect, and the wide open blue of the Aegean is waiting. This could be the summer of our lives.'

She smiled. 'I'm sure it could be. But there will be next summer. We could book the same cruise for our honeymoon.' She stood on tiptoe to kiss his mouth. 'It won't be wasted, darling.'

'It won't be the same,' said Paul in an injured tone.

'No, it won't. We'll be married.'

His frown deepened. 'You don't trust me! That hurts.'

'I don't trust myself. The blue sea, moonlight on deserted decks, all those sunfilled islands the brochure talks

7

about . . .' She laughed. 'Think what we have to look forward to.'

'I'd rather not think about it,' Paul said, his face sulky as a little boy denied a treat. 'Of course, we *could* get married right away, or as soon as possible! And still go on that cruise. Why wait until next year?'

'We could,' she laughed, reaching up once more to kiss him. 'But we won't. Be reasonable, Paul.'

'It's you who is being unreasonable. What's wrong with getting a special licence? We could be married this weekend, be under those gorgeous blue Aegean skies this time next week. Mrs Paul Taylor! Doesn't it sound tempting?'

Kylie, for one crazy moment, felt a sense of bliss attainable just by saying 'yes'. But commonsense took over. She said, 'It sounds wonderful, but we've got the rest of our lives before us, darling. I must—I simply *must*, go out to Umbaya, see the place Daddy loved and slaved for for so long.'

She looked up into his eyes. 'You could come with me. I'm sure the funds would stretch that far.'

But he was shaking his head. 'No. I haven't been in this job long enough to ask for an extended holiday. Remember, the couple of weeks I was due we were going to spend in Greece. But if that's what you really want, Kylie, then go.' His lips twisted. '*I* certainly won't try to stop you.'

Kylie gave a mischievous smile. 'They say absence makes the heart grow fonder, or something, don't they? It'll test our love.'

'I don't need mine testing,' Paul scowled. 'I have complete confidence in my love.' He sighed when she didn't answer and went on, 'Anyway, perhaps it *is* for the best. Give us a chance to straighten out a few ideas. I'll cancel the cruise and put the money back in the savings bank, while you, young lady,' running one finger

8

down the bridge of her nose, 'get this stupid bug out of your system. When do you plan to leave?'

'As soon as I can get a flight. I'll first have to travel down to mother and tell her about it. She doesn't know about the letter, yet. And then see how my boss takes the news.' She shrugged slim shoulders under the cherry red jersey. 'Mind you, I don't really give a damn what he says. I'm still going.'

Paul grinned. 'I do believe, Kylie, you're serious about this.'

His tone held disbelief and she smiled. 'I am serious.'

'Well, this calls for a drink. And, if you're not too busy planning your safari into the wilds, dinner out.'

'I'd love it. Give me an hour to make myself pretty, then we'll have the best night out ever.'

Paul was smiling as he closed the door behind him. Kylie sat down, looking once more at the letter. Inigo J. Beck, Attorney at Law, the letterhead ran. Victory Avenue, Umbaya. The letter itself was brief and formal. As sole inheritor to her father's estate, Mr Beck thought it would be advisable if Miss Graham contact him as soon as possible.

Going into her bedroom she undressed and ran a bath, throwing in a handful of fragrant bathsalts given to her by Paul for Christmas. Relaxing in the warm scented water she let her thoughts drift back—back to her child-hood—to the man who had been her father—to the emerald mine he had named after her mother.

The Sheila Mine! Ever since she was a little girl she had been hearing that name. Like so many men after the last war her father had been torn between the lure of strange places and the land of his birth.

When Kylie was a child she had been fascinated by the pictures his letters conjured up; dark mysterious jungles in which wild animals roamed, free, untamed; towering ranges of purple mountains where waterfalls

9

cascaded in silver perfection; flat, golden veldt country, where wild mimosa grew in abundance between flat-topped 'wait-a-bit' thorn trees that could tear a man or animal to pieces if he tried unwisely to thrust his way through.

He wrote of the sunsets, the trees black against a red and gold sky, streaked with flame-like scarlet ribbons vanishing over the horizon. In her child's mind she saw the jerky gait of a giraffe outlined for a moment as it plucked the topmost foliage, neck stretched long and slim.

She knew about the mine. Not a very large one, but yielding enough to give hope to her father and Tom Kylie, his best friend and after whom she had been named. She looked back, too, over the years, the lonely years spent in England with her mother. Kylie was sixteen when her father discovered the mine. Still Sheila Graham had refused to join her husband in Africa. In spite of their new, more comfortable way of living, the loneliness eventually became too much for her. Especially after Kylie, recently graduated from the expensive secretarial school, had left to take up a post in London and had met Paul Taylor soon afterwards. As though planned the propitous meeting with a middle-aged widower brought new romance to Sheila Graham's life.

If Kylie was shocked when the consultations for divorce came up she did not show it, wishing her mother every happiness, discovering with some dismay that she even liked her mother's new husband-to-be. A discovery that made her feel slightly traitorous to her own father.

It was barely a year after the wedding, her mother, looking delicately lovely in a cream lace gown and large floppy hat, that tragedy struck. Kylie's father, accompanied by his partner, Tom Kylie, had driven into Umbaya, some sixty miles on bad roads, made more treacherous by exceptionally heavy rains.

When they hadn't arrived back by the following morning, Henri Carvalho, their mine manager, sent out search parties. It was days before the two men were found, their car lodged amidst rocks and fallen trees in the fork of a river. Mr Carvalho had written, 'There was no bridge, but they should have known better than to attempt such a crossing. In the dry season it is a simple matter, but with the rains we have recently experienced—very foolish.'

He had ended his long preamble with the words, 'I am heart broken that I should be the one to bring you the news, madam, but there seems no one else . . .'

After reading the letter for the second time her mother had shuddered delicately. 'Well, I certainly don't want anything to do with it, Kylie. All that heat and primitive natives! The dust and flies! Your father knew and understood how I felt about the whole thing. He certainly would not expect me to change my attitude now.'

A week later came the letter from Inigo J. Beck, informing Kylie that, by her father's will, she had inherited the Sheila Mine. Well, the mine may not be worth much, she thought, but she was certainly not going to sell it before first seeing what it was about the place that had held her father and Tom Kylie captives for so long. But more than anything else she wanted to see the country about which her father had written so glowingly. To walk through the dark green jungle and see if the place was really as she had always pictured it. Soon, she told herself, she would know.

TWO

The plane taxied to the end of the narrow runway. The tall grass grew right up to the edge of the tarmac. Kylie could see a corrugated iron structure, its unpainted roof dazzling in the sun's rays and felt in her bag for her dark glasses. The sun was brilliant, an assault on the senses. It must be something to do with the clear air, she thought, and the altitude.

She had learned that Umbaya lay nestled in a range of mountains, the tallest in that part of Central Africa. An African piled the mound of luggage onto a trolley and wheeled it across the soft tarmac. Kylie could feel it sticking to the soles of her thin sandals, feel the white cotton slacks clinging to her legs as she walked. She sighed with relief when at last they entered the cool dimness of the airport buildings.

Customs and immigration took a matter of minutes, then she was in the rather ancient taxi being driven towards town. The driver, a burly African, smiled at her over his shoulder, murmuring reassuringly as they hit the many potholes in a road badly in need of repair.

'It is the rains,' he explained, after one particularly nasty patch had Kylie bobbing from one side to the other like a cork in a bottle. 'The rains have been bad this year.'

The town was not a bit like she had imagined it. She'd seen pictures of tall white buildings, parks ringed with spreading shade trees and bright with beds of vivid flowers. But this conglomeration of rusty, tin-roofed buildings, and shop windows where dead flies and dust seemed the only decoration, made her heart sink and she wondered if, after all, she had been wise in coming.

Perhaps, as Paul said, better to have instructed Mr Beck to sell the mine, enjoy the money . . .

Mr Beck's office, too, when she came to it, was not quite what she expected. It turned out to be one of many, housed in a tall narrow building, the yellowed, once-white paint looking as though it had been applied in Pioneer days and had not been touched since.

And Inigo J. Beck wasn't at all what she had expected, either. He was a tall, very thin man with faded blue eyes and a complexion that spoke of long years in the tropics and numerous doses of malaria. He sat at a desk in an untidy office into which Kylie was shown by an Indian girl in a white sari. She seemed not only to be his secretary but the only member of his staff.

Opposite Mr Beck sat another, much younger man, nonchalant and very much at his ease. Mr Beck introduced her and Kylie felt blue eyes rake her up and down, from the smooth blonde crignon to the dusty white sandals on her feet. 'Miss Graham, I'd like you to meet Steve Jamison. Mr Jamison is your nearest neighbour, up at the mine.'

The man's eyes gave nothing away as he held out a large sun-bronzed hand which Kylie took, feeling its firm coolness in her own. 'How do you do?' she murmured, her own gaze dropping before the cool speculation in his.

'A pleasure, Miss Graham,' he drawled, releasing her hand at last.

He spoke the word cynically, as though to imply he meant just the opposite—or was that just her imagination? She wondered how near a neighbour he would be. Her father had never mentioned any neighbours, to be sure. As though reading her thoughts, the man said, wryly, 'By neighbours, Inigo means we live within twenty-five miles of each other. That, out here, is considered practically next door.'

Kylie gave him a dutiful smile and turned to the lawyer. The young man's attitude hadn't created a good impression with her and she doubted whether further acquaintance would improve it.

'My father's mine,' she began, only to have the lawyer say, as though she hadn't spoken.

'Yes, Mr Jamison owns most of the land that adjoins yours, Miss Graham.'

'How nice for Mr Jamison,' she said frostily, disliking intensely the cool appraising look in the blue eyes. 'If we could discuss my father's . . .'

As though reluctant to discuss the will *or* the mine, Mr Beck went on, smoothly, 'Did you have a good flight, Miss Graham? Travel can be so tiring, I find.'

Kylie took a deep breath. 'Yes, thank you.'

'Do you live in London, Miss Graham?' Steve Jamison gazed at her, taking no notice of her chilly, unsmiling demeanour.

'Yes,' she said, without looking at him.

'Never could stand the place,' Mr Beck said, looking at Steve.

'I find it exciting,' she said, cuttingly.

'Well, everyone to his, or *her* own taste,' Steve Jamison grinned. 'Can't please everyone.'

'You said, in your letter, Mr Beck,' she said, pointedly, 'that you wanted to see me.'

Mr Beck cleared his throat. 'Ah—yes. I thought that as Mr Jamison was in town today you might like to meet someone who will be living close-by. The Sheila Mine is a pretty isolated place—for a woman on her own. You surely do not intend to live there, do you?'

'Yes,' Kylie said. 'Why else would I come all this way, Mr Beck? Of course I mean to live there—until I have

14

decided what to do with the property, anyway.' She looked at the young man coldly. 'It was thoughtful of you to welcome me, Mr Jamison, but I really don't need neighbours.'

Steve Jamison rose, finally getting the hint. 'I'm glad that you feel so confident, Miss Graham. Perhaps, though, when you have met character's like old Saviko you won't feel so opinionated.'

Kylie bristled. Opinionated, indeed! 'Who might he be?' she murmured.

'Saviko?' Was there ridicule in his eyes as he looked at her?

'Saviko is a witchdoctor. He lives in a cave above the Mine. A dangerous man when he is crossed.'

Mr Beck gave a little cough. 'Most unsavoury, Miss Graham. You would do well to stay well clear of him.'

'And yet you say he is living in a cave on *my* property?' Kylie looked from one to the other. Before either man could reply, she went on, crisply, 'Well, then, don't you think he should be moved? What's to *stop* me moving him from my land?'

The two men exchanged glances and Steve grinned, mouth twisting mockingly. 'Saviko is a law unto himself, Miss Graham. I can't see a slip of a girl succeeding in doing what other's have been trying to do for years.'

Kylie's eyes narrowed, the slip-of-a-girl remark an irritant. 'You mean, he would refuse to go even if I ordered him to?'

'I mean just that, Miss Graham. As I said, Saviko is a law unto himself. From what I hear, it is Saviko who gives the orders around the Sheila Mine.'

Rubbish!' Kylie's eyes flashed angrily. 'I'll get the police ...'

'Why don't you wait until you see the place?' Mr Beck interjected in a soothing voice. 'I'm certain you will change your mind about staying once you see how isolated it is.'

He frowned, adding, sternly. 'You would do well to be practical about this whole thing, Miss Graham. It seems to me you are being extremely foolish in being so insistent about it.' Kylie couldn't help but notice the concern in his voice as he spoke. She supposed she should be grateful for the interest he was taking, but, somehow, it irked, this being told what to do and what not to do with her father's dream.

Her lips pursed as he went on, 'I've had a number of offers for the mine, you know, including one from Mr Jamison. He's even offered to pay you more than it is worth. I don't think you should pass it up.'

'Why should anyone offer to pay more than it's worth?' she demanded meeting Steve's eyes challengingly.

'I'd like to add it to my own property.' Steve Jamison had been sitting, listening quietly. Now he stood up, looking at the lawyer. 'You discuss this with Miss Graham, Inigo. I've got to get going. I'm supposed to be getting the month's groceries.' He transferred his gaze to Kylie. 'I'm leaving later for up country. I'd be glad to drive you to the mine.'

'Thank you, Mr Jamison,' she said, coolly. 'But it won't be necessary.'

He shrugged, shook hands with the lawyer and left. Mr Beck frowned at Kylie. 'You should have taken advantage of his offer, Miss Graham.' There was reproach in his voice. 'It isn't easy to get to your father's mine. If you don't mind, my dear, I'd really like to talk to you as I know your father would have done.'

'I *do* mind,' Kylie said, fighting to keep her own voice under control in the face of her mounting anger. 'The man annoyed me. I'd much rather get down to the business that brought me here, Mr Beck.'

16

'But you don't understand!' The man frowned in worried fashion. 'The Sheila . . .' Unable to find the right words he shook his head in disapproval. 'Mr Jamison lives right next to your property. You'd do well to remember he's a pretty important man in this part of the country.'

'I'm impressed!'

'If he wants to buy the place and you won't sell it to him, you might find it impossible to sell to anyone else.'

Kylie drew a deep breath. 'Mr Beck, I really think it is you who does not understand. I don't *want* to sell. I've made up my mind to keep the Sheila Mine.'

The thin mouth tightened. He looked like a petulant child. 'But you've never even seen it!'

'That doesn't matter. I'm going to keep it anyway. Now,' forcing a smile to her lips, 'do you suppose we could get down to business?'

Sighing, he took a long manila envelope from a drawer and opened it. Withdrawing several documents, he riffled through them briefly, then pushed them across his desk towards Kylie. 'There isn't much, I'm afraid. Your father left you the house and the mine. Your mother, I understand, recently remarried?'

Kylie nodded and he went on, 'The house is not in good repair, I'm afraid. Your father and Tom Kylie spent most of their time at the mine. The servants are still there, as well as the mine workers, and, of course, Mr Carvalho and his daughter, who, I believe, housekeeps for him. You'll have the problem of the salaries to meet, but fortunately there are no other debts. Only, of course,' his voice faintly apologetic, 'the legal fees.'

'Oh.' Kylie was silent for a minute or two, looking at him. 'Would you—would you expect your fee straight away, Mr Beck?'

'No—no . . .' he said hastily, waving his hands. 'Your

17

father was well liked in these parts. We don't do business like that out here. I can wait.'

'Thank you. I promise you won't have to wait too long. Is there anything else I should know?'

'Just that you would do well to think again, young lady. The part of the mountains where the Sheila is situated is pretty wild, a long way from anywhere. A young woman on her own could end up in a lot of trouble ...'

He frowned, joining his fingers together at the tips, so that it looked as though he was praying. 'It doesn't do to be too pompous.'

Kylie stood up, reaching for her bag, slipping the strap over one shoulder. Pompous! Really! 'Oh, I don't know, Mr Beck,' she smiled. 'I'm a grown woman. I imagine I can take care of myself.'

She held out her hand for the documents, and reluctantly he gave her the manila envelope. 'I heard about the way you young girls were in England these days,' he said, 'too undisciplined for their own good, but I didn't believe it.'

Kylie smiled, tucking the envelope into her bag. His eyes followed her as she went to the door. One hand on the knob, she turned to say, with genuine gratefulness, 'Thank you for all your efforts, Mr Beck. I really do appreciate all you've done.'

With compressed lips, he said, 'I still insist you are being extremely foolish, Miss Graham. Won't you reconsider?'

'No,' she said firmly. 'There's nothing *to* reconsider,' and smiled as she closed the door, seeing his still shaking head.

In the outer office the Indian girl gazed up from her work on a ledger, dark eyes frankly curious.

'Is there such a thing as a car-hire firm in this town?'

Kylie asked her.

'No.' She looked up at Kylie, head on one side. 'You're trying to get to the M'gisi Heights, aren't you?'

'If that's where the Sheila Mine is, yes I am.'

The girl shook her head. 'There is no way of getting there, if you haven't a car. Only a native bus goes that way.'

'Well, where do I get it and when does it leave?'

The dark eyes widened. 'You would not dare to ride all that way by yourself, in a native bus?' she asked in horror.

'Why not? Is it illegal or something?' Kylie had to smile at the way the girl looked at her. The girl sniffed, as though offended by the question.

'No, of course not. It's just that people—well, *white* people, simply do not ride on native buses. It is—it is not dignified.'

Kylie laughed. 'Dignified or not, if it's the only way I can get to the mine, I'll have to grin and bear it.'

'Well,' the girl shrugged. 'In that case, the bus stop is in the market place. You cannot miss it. Turn right when you leave this building.'

'Thank you,' said Kylie. 'Have you any idea when the next bus leaves?'

Another shrug, bending once more to her work. 'Every few hours, I believe. You should not have long to wait.'

THREE

The market place was easy to find. Kylie just followed the noise. The heat was terrific but once under the trees it was bearable.

There were stalls selling every manner of fruit and vegetable as well as mounds of rice and snowy white maize meal. African women, dressed in lengths of bright cotton and white blouse-like tops, shouted their wares, out-doing each other in clamour. Kylie went over to a wooden bench and placing her suitcase beside her on the dusty ground, sat down. Heaven know's how long she would have to wait but there was much to amuse her in the conglomeration of life all about.

The journey was just beginning to catch up on her and she let herself relax, enjoying the warmth of the sun through the branches above. After about forty minutes a single decker bus drew up. Piled high with all manner of things—wooden boxes, bicycles, wicker-work suitcases, Kylie smiled, seeing a crate of chickens perched perilously on top of everything else. The bus was covered in thick red dust so that the vividly coloured painting on the sides was barely discernable. A crudely done painting of a lion, mouth wide open, showing impossibly long and wicked looking teeth.

The bus trip gave her a better understanding of Mr Beck's reluctance to let her go. The heat and humidity was stifling in the cramped dirty vehicle that was crowded with African passengers of all descriptions. Babies wailed and were fed by their mother's on the spot, openly and not at all discreetly. The smell, too, was overpowering. The smell of dust, oddly perfumed tobacco, the cheap scent that most of the younger women seemed to be drenched in, and unwashed bodies.

The bus made a stop at every village and road-side store as they went deeper into the interior. The range of mountains looming on the horizon seemed to get no nearer. They ground over the deeply pot-holed roads at twenty-five miles an hour and Kylie wondered if, indeed, they would *ever* get there.

When she had got on, to the accompaniment of appraising stares from the other passengers, some puzzled, others frankly antagonistic, the driver, a huge African in a shiny dark uniform and peaked cap, had asked her her destination. He, too, had looked surprised when she'd said the Sheila Mine, but had merely shrugged, taken her money and climbed into his seat behind the wheel.

People got on and off at every stop. No one seemed in any hurry and Kylie thought of her father's letters, his description of the local natives and how time meant very little to any of them. It took almost six hours to negotiate the hundred and odd miles to the stop where the driver turned, and with grinding gears, told Kylie this was the nearest he could take her.

It was now late afternoon, the shadows lengthening, the sun loosing a lot of its heat. Kylie climbed down into the dusty road, was handed her suitcase, a sketchy salute from the driver, and the bus disappeared in a cloud of dust and exhaust fumes. She was the only passenger to alight there. Looking about her all she could see was a ramshackle store. Set back from the road itself, it boasted a narrow wooden verandah supported by two iron poles. Here a cluster of African children crouched, playing some game with bottle tops.

Dogs barked as she approached and the children turned, eyes widening at the sight of the pretty white lady who had arrived as if from nowhere. A red sign, in Eng-

21

lish, announced a popular soft drink. Kylie went into the dark interior of the store, thinking that at least she could quench her thirst before going further. The bus driver had said that the mine was a matter of five or six miles along the narrow turn-off that seemed to lead directly to the foothills of the blue mountains.

A group of men standing to one side of the counter didn't move as she approached them. Merely looked at her with the same antaganism she had noticed on the bus. One leaned over and spat through the door, a stream of evil smelling tobacco that had Kylie wrinkling her nose with distaste.

The gesture made her suddenly aware of the intense silence surrounding her. For a brief moment she felt panic. The dark, blood-shot eyes of the African men were so cold, so openly hostile, that she felt a shiver go through her. She was a stranger in an unfriendly land and it seemed these people were determined she should not forget it.

The African from his position at one end of the counter said, 'The madam wishes something?'

At least, she thought, they were keeping up some semblance of courtesy, if only on the surface. She smiled. 'I'd—I'd like a coke, please.'

'We do not sell drinks.'

'Oh! The sign above your door says different.'

A shrug. 'The sign means nothing. Every store about here possesses such a sign.'

'Then could I have a glass of milk—or water ...?' Seeing how the dark eyes remained unchanged, the expression still openly hostile, she felt in her bag, producing a red leather wallet. 'I'll even pay for a glass of water ...'

The man's eyes fastened on the wallet, greedily and at that same moment a voice from behind them ordered, 'Put that money away!'

22

It was a command that had Kylie spinning on her heel. Steve Jamison filled the doorway, almost blocking out the daylight. The heavy dark brows frowned over those startling blue eyes. They had no right to be so blue, she thought, illogically, in such a dark face.

Transfering his gaze to the storekeeper, his voice was soft as he exclaimed, 'Give the madam a drink.'

The African, although still surly complied quickly, lifting the top of the surprisingly modern deep-freeze cabinet and producing a frosted bottle of orange drink. 'The coke is finished,' he said sulkily, and levered off the top of the bottle, handed it to Kylie.

She forced a friendly smile, a smile that included Steve Jamison.

'Thank you,' she said.

Steve nodded almost imperiously and grunted something she couldn't make out. Feeling the men's eyes fixed on her, Kylie finished the drink and said, 'I've never felt so thirsty in my life. How much do I owe you?'

The storekeeper muttered 'Ten cents' and Kylie paid him. Then she turned to Steve as she heard him say, 'How on earth did you get here, anyway? By bus"

He'd answered his own question and at her nod of assent, went on, 'For God's sake, woman, don't you know how unpleasant that could have been? You really are determined to get that mine, aren't you?'

His lips twitched, making her anger flair. She lifted her chin, staring up at his great height. 'Yes, I am.'

He shrugged. 'Well, looks like you go the rest of the way with me. Come on.' Without more ado he turned, fully expecting her to follow him. When she didn't he paused on the verandah and looked back. His sigh in the hot still afternoon was audible. 'Well, what now? Do you want a lift to the mine or don't you? It's out of my way but it won't kill me.'

23

'How extremely kind of you, Mr Jamison,' she said, icily. 'But I really don't think its necessary.'

His eyes narrowed in a momentary flash of anger, then returned to their normally disinterested expression. 'In that case,' he said, 'I wouldn't dream of forcing you. Good afternoon, Miss Graham.'

He strode across the patch of sunbaked ground between the store and the road, where his Land Rover was parked under the deep shade of a cluster of trees. Before climbing in he looked back once more, seeing her standing hesitantly in the doorway. 'No doubt we'll meet again sometime,' he added, and Kylie thought he sounded as though he couldn't care less.

Two Africans in the back of his Land Rover stirred slightly, welcoming his return with wide smiles, then resumed their afternoon siesta. Kylie felt a sense of desertion overcome her. The African men in the store didn't move. She looked about her in the dark, musty interior, and noticed how their eyes followed Steve as he climbed into the Land Rover. Then one of the men, thick-set and dressed in dirty dungerees, nodded and said something to the others.

Their words came to Kylie in a mumble of unintelligible sound. One grinned and the thick-set man moved, approaching Kylie slowly and she felt panic overtake her. A fear that she had never experienced before. The stench of the man was overpowering in the confines of the small store. With a gasp she turned and ran, covering the dusty floorboards and was out on the verandah and across the road before she could think.

Behind her the men guffawed, then she felt a hand helping her into the Land Rover and an amused voice saying, 'Changed your mind, did you?'

Refusing to be drawn, she sat rigid, staring straight ahead, while beside her Steve Jamison engaged gears.

24

The Land Rover coughed, backfired and moved smoothly onto the road. After a moment or two during which Kylie felt the tense, frightened muscles beginning to relax a little, Steve looked sideways at her, eyes twinkling. She tensed again, an angry retort on her lips, expecting some brilliant piece of sarcasm, but sensing her mood he kept silent.

The track deteriorated as they entered the foothills, huge rocks and sometimes boulders appearing in front of them. Steve drove with a fierce concentration that Kylie could not help but admire, avoiding somehow the worst of the ruts and bumps in the road. Once, changing into bottom gear, he slowed almost to a standstill to negotiate a dry river bed. The rains of a few weeks ago might almost have been just a memory, now just a few damp patches in the sand below them. Kylie tried in vain to imagine how it must have been with the river a swirling torrent, eager to trap the unwary. Of her father and Tom Kylie battling for their lives in its midst . . .

But she pushed the thoughts from her mind. It was too painful, too recent. Better to think of the future, and immediately after that she found her whole attention centered on the way Steve drove the Land Rover shuddering up the other side of the river bed. She hung on with both hands and Steve turned to grin at her. 'All right?'

She nodded, feeling completely dwarfed by the range that rose before them, the majestic sweep of escarpment. Ever upwards, the road twisted and turned. The panoramic views were breathtaking. At a place where the road widened, Steve brought the vehicle to a halt. 'We'll take a breather,' he said, taking it for granted that Kylie would be entirely in agreement. Actually, she was so relieved to step down on firm ground once more, after the hair-raising drive, that she would have agreed to anything. She nodded, feeling her ears singing in the sudden silence after the rattling, whining ascent of the Land Rover. Below them the whole countryside sparkled with the vivid green foliage brought on by the first rains, and far away to the west Kylie noticed a valley clothed completely in hues ranging from pale pink, through all the oranges to bloodred and scarlet to deep mahogany.

'How perfectly lovely!' she breathed. 'What are they?'

'Msasa trees. Most of the year they are pretty insignificant. Now, of course, you're seeing them at their best. It's that time of the year.'

Kylie stood at the edge of the road, and tucked her hands, thumbs out, in the pockets of the white denim jeans she was wearing and surveyed the valley. The wind caught at her hair, dislodging stray ends from the usually tidy crignon she wore, blowing them into her eyes and mouth. Steve's eyes were amused. 'Tie your scarf about your head,' he advised, and before she could remove the silk scarf from where it was tucked into the neck of her yellow silk shirt, he'd pulled it free, and with calm, unhurried fingers was knotting the ends under her chin. Standing back, he smiled down at her. 'There, that's better, isn't it?'

She nodded, acutely conscious of his cool fingers as they touched her neck. Once more they turned their eyes towards the glorious show put on by nature, and Steve went on, 'Of course, these mountains are sacred, you know. The Africans say they are taboo.'

She laughed, an unsteady little laugh that betrayed just how tired she was, and glancing at her sharply he said, with a curtness that made her frown, 'Okay, come on, up with you. Mustn't waste time.'

He gave her a little push and she sank back onto the hard, unsprung leather seat, thinking of his words— 'The Africans say these mountains are taboo', remembering how she felt at first sight of the country through the windows of the hot, dirty bus. A sense of hidden, threatening things, a menace that the brilliant sun streaming over the thick, tropical bush could not hide.

Her reflections were interrupted by an exclamation from the man at her side. She jerked her eyes upwards to meet his. 'Sorry, I was dreaming . . .'

'I said, if I hadn't come along, would you really have walked all this way?'

'If I had to.'

'You are a very determined young lady.' His eyes teased. 'Or maybe stubborn would fit the description better.'

'Paul says that too.'

His eyebrows lifted. 'Paul?'

'My fiancé.'

'Your fiancé!' His tone was incredulous. 'And he let you come all this way on your own?'

'Yes.' Now Kylie's eyes teased. 'You *said* I was a very determined young lady.' Then suddenly she was serious. 'You see, it was impossible for him to take enough time off to accompany me. He'd only just started this job . . .'

'I don't see how it could possibly have mattered. He'll be coming out to join you, won't he? If you intend to stay, that is.'

'I intend to stay, Mr Jamison. Have no doubts about that.'

A shrug. 'That's your indaba . . . Ah, here we are.'

He made a right turn, throwing her against him. Grinning in that infuriating fashion, he brought the Land Rover to a halt, saying, 'There's the house, over there.'

The range of hills that rose behind, their slopes covered in the glorious reds and pinks of the msasas, made a magnificent background. All the same, the sight of the unprepossessing cluster of buildings made most of her en-

27

thusiasm fade. Made of wood, many years ago, the house was shabby, badly in need of a coat of paint, with a rusty corrugated iron roof and a sagging verandah held up by wooden stakes from underneath. Kylie thought, one good push and the whole thing would collapse!

As Steve leaped to the ground, then held out one hand to assist her, she could see tatty cane chairs and tables grouped on the verandah, screened by a creeper with blue trumpet shaped flowers. The whole place looked incredibly sleazy and she turned to catch Steve's eye, her own bright with disenchanted tears. Giving an attempt at a laugh, more to hide the sudden anger he felt than anything else, Steve said, 'Welcome home!'

His eyes searched for signs of life. But the whole place slumbered in its afternoon siesta, a fact that annoyed him even further. Was there *on one* to meet the girl?

The sound of the Land Rover's engine, ticking in the stillness, was loud and it was impossible to believe that the house had not been deserted for years. Kylie stood below the verandah, reluctant to climb the rickety steps leading up to the house. Steve said, 'Seems everyone is resting. Hold on a minute, I'll see if I can ...'

Before he could finish footsteps were heard crossing the verandah floor above them and the screen door was pushed open. A girl stood there, olive-skinned, lovely, her raven hair parted in the centre and falling to her shoulders in a careless but effective way. She wore a scarlet patterned frock, tightly fitting, calculated to show off the shape of her body. She could, Kylie decided, have been any age between sixteen and twenty-six. Her mouth was a careless crimson slash of lipstick, applied obviously in a hurry at the sound of the visitors. Her eyes, dark, like brown velvet, stared down at them. For a moment, Kylie stared back at her.

'Hello!' she said, and smiled at Steve, after the first long look ingoring Kylie.

Kylie said, 'You are . . . ?'

'Anna Marie Carvalho.' She smiled again, showing perfect white teeth, and came down the verandah steps slowly. 'You cannot be Miss Graham?'

Kylie felt her anger stir, slowly, heatedly at the girl's almost disdainful manner. 'Why couldn't I be?'

The girl wrinkled her nose and smiled at Steve, then gave Kylie a long, cold look. 'Because you are not expected. My father said nothing of your arrival.'

Kylie's lips tightened. The tears that had threatened a few minutes ago now completely forgotten and anger taking their place, she said, 'Perhaps you would be good enough to show me into the house. I've had rather a long and tiring journey.'

'But of course!' The girl stood to one side, then raised her voice, to call, 'Poppy, you lazy slut! Come here and take Miss Graham's things.'

An African girl came forward. She bobbed a cursty then took Kylie's suitcase from Steve. 'I'll see that your room is ready,' Anna Marie murmured and followed the maid along the corridor, Steve's eyes following the deliberately cultivated swaying walk with such intentness that Kylie had to smile, in spite of her anger.

'Who is she, do you suppose?' she asked. 'And what's she doing here, living in this house . . . ?'

Steve laughed and felt with two fingers into his top shirt pocket for his packet of cigarettes. 'Her name, if I recall correctly, is Anna Marie Carvalho, and it would appear she is the daughter of your mine manager and so lives here with her father.'

Enraged still further by his calm, almost teasing manner, Kylie said, 'I don't *mean* that. Oh, you *know* what I mean. Why is she here, living in a place like this?

Surely she is the sort of girl who would prefer the bright lights of some city. I wouldn't say this was her scene, would you?'

'Perhaps she *wants* to be with her father,' Steve murmured and then was silent as the girl came back. She joined them and dropped into a cane chair nearby. She drew up her legs under her and smiled at Steve. 'You have some English cigarettes, no? I have not smoked an English cigarette for months.'

Carefully avoiding Kylie's eyes, Steve leaned forward in his chair, offering the girl the packet. 'Be my guest!'

There was a short silence while Anna Marie puffed at her cigarette, looking appreciatively at Steve and fluttering her eyelashes. Unable to stand it a moment longer Kylie said, 'Perhaps you would be good enough to tell me where everyone is?'

'By everyone,' the girl murmured, 'I suppose you mean my father.'

She shrugged, slim shoulders moving under the skimpy red and white dress. It had a low neckline and Kylie noticed how deeply tanned she was.

She puffed deeply at her cigarette and her face became mockingly grave. 'My father is working. He spends the whole day and most of the evening in the office at the mine face.'

Steve stood up. 'I'll have to go, Miss Graham. It'll be dark soon and I don't fancy being out after dark on these roads.' Hesitating briefly, he added, 'Will you be all right?'

Kylie nodded. 'Of course. I'll be fine. And thanks for everything. I'm—I'm sorry I was so abrupt with you at first ...'

She waved goodbye as he got into the Land Rover. Then she followed Anna Marie back into the house. At a bedroom door the dark girl stood back, allowing Kylie to enter first. 'You know,' she said, eyeing Kylie with a look that held no warmth, no friendship, or even liking. 'You know, you are very much like your father, Miss Graham. Oh, not in looks, but in the manner he loved to use with people. People that he considered inferior to himself.'

Kylie turned to face her. 'I don't know what you mean. My father was a very fair man. He would never be abrupt or tyranical with anyone, especially one of his own employees.'

The girl shrugged. Then she said, 'I hope you will find everything you want here. Dinner is usually at seven-thirty, when my father returns from the mine.'

For a long moment they stood looking at each other, then the girl closed the door, leaving Kylie alone. Looking about her Kylie sucked in her breath with shocked disappointment. The colour scheme of the room was dreary, the furniture sparse and made of heavy red timber. The curtains hung listlessly, their once vibrant orange faded in patches by the sun. Then her natural optimism returned and she told herself a good scrubbing, followed by some fresh paint would work wonders.

She thought of her father, and a certain loyalty to his memory told her that it would take more than a dreary bedroom to drive her away. Or, wryly, a girl with dark eyes and a coolly calculated arrogance.

She sat down heavily on the bed. The springs gave a disgruntled sound and she smiled. After a few moments she pushed open the door leading to the bathroom, peering inside. Even though the huge hot water tank was perched perilously above the yellow stained bath, she ran the hot water, undressing and soaking away all the aches and pains of the long bumpy ride. Then dressing quickly in a clean dress of thin white cotton patterned with yellow daisies, she brushed her hair until it fell across

31

her shoulders in golden waves.

Far too hot to wear it loose, she twisted it into its usual tidy crignon and then thrusting her bare feet into thronged sandals wondered back onto the verandah.

FOUR

Dinner was served by candlelight and Kylie felt the empty uncomfortable feeling in her middle give way to a sleepy well-being and she told herself she might even enjoy living here, in this ramshackle building that had been her father's last home.

Her lids felt heavy and it became increasingly more difficult to keep them open. They heard the sound of a motor outside in the driveway and Anna Marie jumped up, throwing her napkin down on the table beside her.

'My father has arrived! No doubt,' looking sharply at Kylie, 'he will be surprised to see you.'

Kylie's mouth twitched. 'No doubt!'

The big man paused at the door, gazing at Kylie with something like consternation while his daughter murmured introductions. Then with a wide welcoming smile he hurried forward, hands outstretched. 'Miss Graham! So nice to meet you at last. I'm only sorry I was not here to greet you. Please forgive us, though. We had no idea you were coming so soon. Mr Beck thought next month sometime.'

He seated himself opposite the two girls and Anna Marie took his plate, filling it with roast guinea fowl and new potatoes that Kylie found so delicious. Proceeding to eat, he said, 'I will take you on a tour of exploration tomorrow. We'll go early, before it becomes too hot.' He held her gaze, his dark eyes seeming to bore right into her. 'Miss Graham' he said in a low voice. 'May I ask you to be completely frank with me?'

'Of course,' Kylie replied quickly.

'Do you intend to keep the Sheila Mine?'

B

'Yes, I do.'

Watching, Kylie saw the look that was exchanged between father and daughter. Saw the sudden relief in the faces. It was as if they had been freed of some oppressive burden.

'Then our biggest problem is taken care of,' he said.

'I don't understand, Mr Carvalho?'

He shrugged. 'The important thing is that you want to stay here. If you're going to keep the mine, we can manage.' Seeing Kylie's look of perplexity, he added, 'The mine had fallen off a bit, you know. Wasn't paying as well as it should do, and we were having all sorts of trouble with the workers.'

'Saviko?' she heard herself say, abruptly.

He gave her a curious stare. 'How did you know about Saviko?'

'Steve—Mr Jamison told me. Isn't he some kind of witchdoctor?'

Mr Carvalho nodded. 'He is. And the boys are frankly terrified of him.'

Kylie gazed at him, a tight little smile playing about her lips. 'Well, we'll have to see about that. The first thing we must do is evict him from my land.'

She heard the sound of Anna Marie's soft laugh as her father said, 'You sound just like Tom Kylie. Things didn't always go well with him and your father, but they always tried.'

'Thank you,' Kylie told him. 'From what I know of both of them, I consider that a compliment.'

She woke in the night to the sound of drums—a constant thud—thud that seemed to make the whole room vibrate with their curious rhythm. For a long time she lay listening. Then silence fell and the only sounds were the night ones of wind and leaves and birds twittering. She was wide awake long before Poppy brought her tea the next morning. The air seemed unexpectedly cool and fresh and she felt excitement overtake her.

Hastily she pulled on slacks and a shirt and twisting her hair up out of the way she ran along the corridor to the dining room. Poppy was just putting out bowls of fresh fruit—slices of paw paw, banana and orange segments and smiled her goodmorning. She indicated the tall silver coffee pot, saying, 'The coffee is hot, madam. You wish some now?'

It was, hot and refreshing and while she was pouring her second cup, Mr Carvalho appeared. He seemed surprised to see her up and dressed so early, but she told him she was eager to see the mine and its surroundings, wanting to know exactly how large her domain was and how many workers they employed.

'My father was so awfully vague in his letters,' she said, smiling. 'I haven't a clue about how big the mine is or anything, or how many emeralds you produce.'

'The best week's production at the mine has been just over 200 grams, the worst only 20 grams,' Mr Carvalho told her. 'It's been a struggle at times, rising costs, transport difficulties, but we survived. If you've finished your breakfast, I'll show you.' He gazed down at her feet, nodding in approval when he saw the sensible walking shoes she wore. 'It's a rough climb,' he explained, 'Anna never goes up there if she can possibly help it.'

Kylie followed him from the house. The track he took was badly rutted, baked by the sun into a concrete-like hardness. The red dust rose in little puffs about their feet as they walked and soon the blue jeans and white shirt Kylie wore were covered in the stuff. The long grass bent and whispered all about them. Sudden rustlings at the side of the path, telling of small creatures disturbed by their passing, made Kylie start nervously. 'Are—are there any snakes, or anything?' she murmured at one

35

such time, seeing what she imagined was the green oily sheen of a snake's back as it moved away at their approach.

'If there are, they don't usually hang around. The sound of our footsteps would scare them away, or rather, the vibration. Never forget, if you plan to live in this country, that they are usually more afraid of you than you are of them.'

Kylie's nose wrinkled in comical fashion. 'Wanna bet?'

The manager laughed. They continued their way upwards and after a while Kylie paused to catch her breath. 'Phew, is it always as hot as this?'

'Not always. Once the rains start it can get very cold. Log fires at night and extra blankets on your bed.'

A thought suddenly struck her. She said, 'Did you hear the drums during the night, Mr Carvalho? It was —eerie, wasn't it?'

He looked away to where the sun turned the hillside into a blaze of scarlet and gold, shining on the leaves of the msasas. He seemed, she thought, to be deliberately avoiding her eyes. 'It was nothing, Miss Graham. The boys celebrating some wedding, or perhaps the birth of a baby son to one of their wives.'

Hesitantly, she murmured, 'It didn't seem like that kind of—of celebration, Mr Carvalho. More like a warning . . .'

Still he avoided her eyes. 'I'll ask them. They use the drums as a bush telegraph, you know. Probably the news of your arrival.'

She looked at him. 'Why should anyone be interested in my arrival? Anyone but my own mine workers, I mean?'

But he was already moving, away from her on the upward path, as though he wanted to hear no more of the subject. Flushing a little—for wasn't he still one of her employees? Kylie followed. It took them about thirty minutes to reach the mine workings, by which time she felt completely drained of energy. She noticed immediately the groups of African workers who stood about. Machinery was scattered everywhere on the dusty ground and the air was filled with the noise of it, a heavy thud-thud that disrupted the birds nesting in the msasa trees all about.

She followed the mine manager to a tiny corrugated office where a young man sat, working over a ledger. He raised dark eyes as they entered, Mr Carvalho introducing Kylie. The young man, dark, very good-looking, murmured his pleasure. Kylie guessed he would be Italian for he was introduced as Vito Versini. Later Mr Carvalho took her around the compound where the workers lived. There was a lot of laughter and noise, but Kylie was horrified to see the state of the children's clothing, the bundled-up babies on the women's backs, the flies that crawled into their eyes and mouths.

'Is there no clinic for the women and babies? No school for the older children?'

'No.' Mr Carvalho looked at her. His face was expressionless. 'If anything happened that your father or Mr Kylie could not handle, they would be taken in the mine truck to town. Otherwise, they manage by themselves.'

His smile was kind. 'They always have, you know. They put more faith into one of Saviko's remedies than anything we could give them.'

As he spoke he gazed up at the hillside above them. Clothed in the pinks, russets, scarlets and lime-greens of the msasa it was an inspiring sight. And, thought Kylie, in the midst of it all, Saviko, the witchdoctor, and all the savagery of an Africa of long ago . . .

37

Mr Carvalho was still speaking. 'The mine boys and their families put great faith in what he says. His predictions, especially.'

'Predictions?' Kylie frowned, puzzled at the man's tone.

'Yes. Saviko predicted, for instance, that if your father went ahead developing the Sheila, particularly that piece of ground on the side of the hill that used to be a burial ground, he would come to harm. Scarcely a month later the accident happened . . .'

Kylie stared at him open mouthed. 'Are you trying to tell me that this—this witchdoctor had something to do with my father's death?'

Breaking into her words the sound of an argument came loud on the still air. They saw a group of men beginning to tussle with each other, then the young Italian appeared, running over to them and attempting to part the fighters. Mr Carvalho said, 'I must go. Will you be able to find your way back, Miss Graham? I shouldn't hang around too long, if I were you. Once they get going, anything can happen.'

Kylie hesitated. But the blazing heat of the sun seemed as though it was having a dehydrating effect upon her. She could feel the perspiration running down her back inside her shirt, feel it wetting her hair at the temples. 'All right,' she agreed, although Mr Carvalho recognized reluctance in her voice. 'Perhaps I have had enough for one morning.'

'Good girl. Sure you can manage?'

Kylie nodded. As she walked back along the narrow track leading to the house she was aware of being watched. She turned to see a figure slip behind a group of trees. It seemed impossible that the conversation they had just had—witchdoctors and curses, could really have taken place. This was Africa, agreed. But twentieth century Africa. Independence and all that! Surely such things didn't still happen?

Returning to the blessed shade of the verandah she found Anna Marie stretched out in a long cane chair. She smiled as Kylie came onto the verandah, her dark eyes resting on the English girl's sun-flushed face.

'You *have* been indiscreet, Miss Graham! Too much sun is not good. My father should have warned you.'

There was a small silence while Poppy hurried forward with a glass for Kylie. Orange juice in which ice-cubes tinkled.

Rising from her chair Anna Marie stretched and said, 'I am going to swim before lunch. Do you want to join me?'

'Sounds just the thing.' Kylie looked pointedly at the rather over-grown garden, the patchy lawn. 'But where?'

'We have a pool at the back. Not much of a one, but it is sufficient.'

The pool was large and square and the sides were covered in a green, moss-like substance. Built as it was beneath tall spreading trees the water took on the olive greenness of the foliage, looking slightly sinister. Nevertheless its icy waters felt deliciously cool after the rather hot climb and Kylie caught herself thinking that perhaps living here wasn't going to be so bad after all. After a brisk swim Anna Marie arranged herself in a red and white canvas deckchair and shook the water from her long hair. Her eyes were intent on Kylie as she swam the length of the pool, pushed herself away from the far end and then swam lazily back.

Towelling the drops of water from her deeply tanned legs, Anna Marie said, her voice drawling, 'What exactly are your plans, Miss Graham? Oh, I know you intend to keep the mine on, but surely you don't mean to live here, alone?'

Resting her forearms on the edge of the pool, Kylie looked at her.

'If it's anything to do with you, and I don't think it has, my fiancé is going to join me here and we are going to get married.' Her voice sounded coolly amused, but inside she felt anything but. Anna Marie's whole attitude annoyed her. Why, she wondered, should the other girl resent her so?

She added, her voice taking on a determination that seemed to disconcert the dark girl, '*And* we're going to make this place pay. With Paul by my side, I'd just like to see anyone try and stop me.'

As she walked across the cool stone verandah, leaving wet imprints of her bare feet, Kylie found a spring in her step that had been missing lately.

'You're very much the Grand Dame, Kylie Graham,' she told herself as she changed from her wet bathing suit into a cotton dress for lunch. 'Maybe that's easy when you're ignorant of the job ahead of you! Here's your father slaving for close on twenty years to make a fortune and you're going to do it all at once! Let's hope you don't end up by looking foolish, or worse . . . !'

She didn't know how long she'd been asleep when the sounds woke her. The sounds of heavy breathing, of a strange thudding that seemed to be right inside her head, and a voice, murmuring incantations in a voice creaking with age. Sounds that, when she sat up, seemed to be formed of the very air. But, after listening intently for a few minutes, sounds she could definitely hear. But not the drum sounds of the other night, she decided. Definately not drum sounds.

Instinctively, she clutched the blanket to her breast and stared wide-eyed into the darkness. It wasn't a dream. The sounds were there, almost beside her in the dark room. She remembered herself scoffing at the possibility of Saviko and his magic, and it was as though icy fingers slid down her spine.

But, pulling herself together, she told herself that was pure nonsense. The sounds were real. Throwing back the bedclothes, she felt for her slippers. She slipped her feet into them and padded to the window, peering out into the silent night. At once the sounds stopped. She turned, leaning against the window sill, listening. But they had gone and with them the sense of evil that before seemed to permeate the very air she breathed.

The room remained quiet and she went back to bed, pulling the covers over her head, unaccountably shivering now that it was over. After a while she fell asleep, and dreamed strange, formless dreams in which fire writhed, and a tall, thin man dressed in animal skins and some hideous mask whom she saw briefly through the tremulous flames.

Once again in the night she woke. There were no flames, no sounds. All was calm and quiet. This time she fell asleep and did not waken until Poppy knocked at the door with her morning tea.

B*

FIVE

At breakfast Kylie looked at Mr Carvalho and his daughter and said, abruptly, 'Did either of you hear strange noises last night?'

'What kind of noises, Miss Graham?' Mr Carvalho looked at her strangely.

'Like the sound of a drum beating, and a voice mumbling ... It was difficult to tell where they came from, but it seemed as though they were right in my room with me.' Realizing how foolish it sounded, Kylie pulled a face, her lips twisting. 'It wasn't like the other night, just drums. It—it was *weird*.'

The mine manager stiffened. 'No, I don't remember hearing anything, Miss Graham.'

'Oh,' Kylie said, and transferred her gaze to Anna Marie, who said, mockingly, 'Perhaps you were dreaming, Miss Graham.'

'I wasn't. I even got out of bed and went to the window. I wasn't dreaming.'

The dark girl's lips twisted in a sarcastic smile. 'My, how very brave!'

It was obvious that she would get no help from that direction, especially when Mr Carvalho went on, 'Sometimes, in a strange house, our nerves play tricks on us. Especially the first few nights.'

Kylie met his eyes squarely. 'Perhaps so,' she said, and rose from the table. 'I think I'll take a walk up the hill.'

Mr Carvalho looked up from his breakfast. 'Want me to come with you?'

Kylie shook her head. If she had to get used to doing things on her own, at least until Paul was able to join her, let her start as she meant to go on. The track this morning didn't seem nearly as rough and she found herself actually enjoying the walk. Approaching storm clouds effectively muted the sun's brilliance and she noticed how the glorious shades of the trees stood out glowingly against the darkening sky. Mr Carvalho had mentioned the possibility of rain, so she must not be too long.

Approaching the tiny corrugated iron office where the young Italian worked, she was once again aware of the groups of workers standing about, seemingly at a loose end. She must speak to Mr Carvalho about this, she thought. Why, for heaven's sake, weren't they working? She felt their eyes boring into her back as she entered the office. Vito leaped to his feet at her appearance, flushing as she gave him a friendly smile. 'Good morning, Vito! Busy?'

'Always busy, Miss Graham.'

She looked about her; a desk by the window, a filing cabinet and typewriter with an angle-lamp above it, for in spite of the window the light was not good. Looking at him, she said, 'If there is anything I can do to help, I'll be glad to. Filing, some typing maybe . . . ?'

'Not to worry, Miss Graham. We manage, Mr Carvalho and myself, to take care of these things.'

He looked as though he had been entering the ledger and Kylie smiled, saying, 'Well, if you're sure there is nothing I can do . . .' and made good her escape, glad to be out in the fresh air again after the humid stuffiness of the tiny office. She wondered where Vito lived, and reminded herself to ask Mr Carvalho. As she crossed the dusty compound the women watched her approaching, their dark eyes strangely blank and she wondered if she *would* be able to do anything for them. Small children clung to their mother's skirts and watched with huge eyes as she came nearer. The bigger ones ran inside their

43

huts, and shouted to each other in shrill voices in which alarm and belligerence was plainly evident.

One tiny tot, no more than two years old, staggered across her path, on its way to join a bigger sister. It wore a string of beads beneath its protruding tummy and Kylie smiled, holding out one hand towards it. The child screamed; shrill wails that had every mother in sight turning, running towards it. Suddenly the compound was empty, the huts silent, the tightly closed doors gazing back at her like malevolent eyes.

A feeling of hopelessness overtook Kylie. She sighed and turned, to continue up the hill. This was going to be more difficult than she imagined! After a few yards she stopped to catch her breath and gazed behind her, down into the valley. It was beautiful! How her father must have loved it! His visits to his family now understandably brief *because* of his affection for this land.

A big bird, startled by her progress, fluttered clumsily from a tree overhead and vanished with an eerie, hollow cry. Once her heart had returned to normal she patted the beads of perspiration on her upper lip, and wondered if she hadn't been foolish, coming all this way up the hill by herself.

On the point of turning back she saw the cave on the hillside above her, the man sitting like a black monolith outside its entrance. He was watching her carefully and for a brief moment she hesitated, then lifting her chin, went to meet him.

He looked like an agile monkey, she thought, crouching there in the cave mouth. A wiry-looking individual with a shaved head and pierced earlobes through which enormous pieces of bone had been forced. But what frightened her more than anything else was his smile, for all the front teeth in his upper jaw had been filed to points.

44

Feeling her heart resume its thudding, she nevertheless stood her ground and returned his gaze. Then, trying to ignore the dryness in her throat, she said in a low voice, 'Good morning!'

Without preamble, his voice a high thin wail, he answered, 'Go away, Kylie Graham! You are not wanted here.'

'How do you know who I am?' Kylie's own voice shook but she was not going to be intimidated by this old man, even if the African women in the compound had repulsed her first offers of friendship.

'I know! I know many things! I know how your father and his friend were killed and even if I *had* been able to warn him I would not have done so.'

He shrugged thin shoulders under the dark blanket he wore. It seemed astonishing to Kylie that his English was so good and she persisted, stubbornly, her first feelings of alarm beginning to fade. 'What had you against my father, against me, Saviko? What harm did my father ever do you?'

His chuckle echoed over the lonely hillside. 'So you know my name, too, Miss Graham? They have been talking about me in the compound?'

There was a question in his voice. Kylie shook her head. 'No. The only things I know about you are what I have been told by others.'

'And that is ... ?'

'That not only are you trespassing on my land, but you are also terrorizing my workers and their families into accepting all sorts of foul remedies that would probably do more harm than good, besides coercing them into idleness.'

Once more his chuckle rung out, vicious, satanic in the quiet peacefulness of this lovely hillside. It died away, followed by a silence that seemed to throb in Kylie's ears.

Suddenly she felt more frightened than she had ever felt in her life.

'If you do not go, leave the mine alone,' she heard herself cry, 'I will be forced to get the police to you.'

His lips curled contemptuously and he spat on the ground at her feet.

'The white people will give up the mine, give up the plans your father made for desecrating our sacred burial ground. The police can do nothing. I am Saviko. Nothing can harm me, not even the white peoples' police force.'

His voice dropped to a hiss. 'If the man who came with you wishes to speak with me, I will listen. To no other. I do not speak with women.'

'You would speak to Steve Jamison?' Kylie stared at him. 'How did you know he came with me? Or,' sarcastically, 'is there nothing the great Saviko does not know?'

Giving her one last, contemptuous look, he rose to his feet, gathering the dark blanket about him and stood looking down at her. Then leaning slightly forward, he approached across the leaf-littered ground, his red-rimmed eyes never once leaving her face. For the first time Kylie felt a little less sure of her ground. Holding her breath, she watched him approach, to stop within a few feet. He began to speak rapidly in his own tongue, a rambling dialogue that sounded to the trembling girl wildly threatening.

Then, as though to intimidate her still further, he began to act out a pantomime. First of all there where two men in a car. It was amazing how he conveyed the men, the vehicle stranded in the middle of a flooding river, to be washed away swiftly downstream, twisting and turning in the angry current . . .

Kylie felt herself go cold. There was no mistaking the

story he told. Or the one that followed; a man and a woman, somewhere in a desolate place, danger between them and safety. Kylie was left in no doubt that the woman was to be herself. And the man—Paul?

After his voice died away, the silence strung itself out on a nerve-taut thread. Then the man suddenly drew himself to his full height. So sudden was his movement that she screamed. Holding his arms straight out from his side, the blanket flapping like the wings of some giant bat, he lunged at her and Kylie, nerve completely gone by now, screamed again and turned to run.

Blindly she stumbled back down the rocky hillside, ankles turning on the stones. Behind her, she heard Saviko's laugh ring out, high and mocking.

Then the only sounds were her own sobbing breath and the shrill protesting of the birds as she ran through the trees. She glanced back over her shoulder, convinced that the old man must be following her. But there was no one. Only the msasas moved in the wind, their colours merging into a glorious medley of reds and pinks . . .

She almost screamed again as a hand came out and gripped her arm. It was Steve Jamison. 'Where's the fire?' he grinned. 'Isn't it a bit hot to be tearing around like this?'

'Oh, God! Steve,' she gasped, her headlong rush halted by his body. He stood solidly in the pathway before her and his voice suddenly was the most beautiful and re-assuring sound she had ever heard. 'It was—that Saviko, the witchdoctor Mr Beck told us about. He's—he's up there,' pointing upwards through the trees.

Steve frowned, gazing to where she pointed. 'Did he harm you?'

'No. Just frightened the daylights out of me. He said —oh, all sorts of horrible things, Steve—things about my father and Tom, about their deaths . . .' A wave of

47

sickness seemed to rise up in her throat and she leaned against him, grateful for the comfort of his arms as they closed about her. She closed her eyes and the sun-filled hillside was blotted out.

But her closed eyelids retained the molten scarlet of the msasas, red like blood, and she shivered, remembering Saviko's pantomime ...

'Look, why don't you wait here and I'll go up and have a word with him?' Steve held her away at arms length, gazing down into her eyes. Kylie drew a deep breath, hesitating. Then nodded. 'All right. Perhaps you should. He said he would talk to you. But,' smiling wryly, 'You're not leaving me here alone. I'm coming with you.'

The old witchdoctor sat as though he hadn't moved, sunning himself like a lizard. 'You wanted to speak with me, madala?' Steve began, dropping to his haunches a few yards away.

The old man nodded. 'I did. You realize, Steve Jamison, I am not afraid of your white police, and no black man would dare lay hands on me. This you and the woman will discover if you try to move me from this place.'

Steve lit a cigarette and inhaled deeply and at the old man's, 'I, too, smoke the white man's cigarettes', approached closer and offered him the packet. Kylie gasped with indignation as the old man chuckled and a skinny arm shot out from the folds of the blankets and grasped the packet, holding it to himself as would a child with a new toy.

Steve laughed, to her further indignation, and said, 'All right. You old reprobate, you can keep it.'

Saviko added his quiet laugh to Steve's, his eyes on Kylie where she stood a few yards away, eyes wide with shock at the seeming friendship between the two men. The witchdoctor said, looking now at Steve, 'It is possible that the pale-haired one and yourself would be very contented together, Steve Jamison. I will work towards it for you.' He shot Steve a keen look. 'You would wish it, no?'

Once more Steve laughed. 'No! The pale-haired one has other plans. Save your breath, old man. Now,' a frown taking the place of the former good-humoured smile, 'if that is all you have to say to me that is important, I will be going.'

The old limb of Satan! he thought. Working towards a union between himself and Kylie! The idea was so attractive that he almost felt compelled to say, 'Fair enough, old man! See what you can do.'

Grinning at the thought, so tempting, so ridiculous, he said instead, 'You will not frighten the pale-haired one any more, you hear me! She has inherited from her father and what went before has nothing to do with her.'

His frown deepened, and there was a warning in his voice as he added, 'If I hear that you, Saviko, have harmed her in any way, either by words or actions, I will come with the police and you will spend the next five years in prison in Umbaya. You understand what I am telling you, old man?'

Saviko nodded, and although Kylie did not understand what they said, for they had fallen into local lialect, she could have sworn she saw sudden respect in the old witchdoctor's eyes.

Later at the house, sipping the cool orange juice Poppy brought, Kylie said, 'What did he say? That bit at the end, when he seemed to turn all ingratiating?'

Steve laughed into her eyes. 'Nothing much. A lot of rubbish that boiled down meant precisely nothing. He may be dangerous, but I think he's past his prime. I shouldn't worry too much if I were you, Kylie.'

Kylie gazed at him wide-eyed. 'But all those things

he told me? About my father and Mr Kylie ... ?'

'Saviko has a gift of the gab that would make him a fortune in London or some other big city, Kylie. Most of it is auto-suggestion. He has that down to a T, a gift for influencing the mind in what he *wants* you to believe. And, let's face it, the things he predicted had already happened, so all he had to do was get your imagination working and you would do the rest yourself.'

At Kylie's look of disbelief, he went on, wryly, 'Saviko could show a trick or two to some of *our* tame psychologists, believe me, Kylie.'

Grudingly, she murmured, 'You may be right, Steve.'

He poured himself another drink. Saviko was harmless, he told himself. If there had been the slightest doubt in his mind about that, he would see to it in Umbaya that the matter was properly investigated. Saviko would be charged under the Suppression of Witchcraft Act. As it was, he felt Kylie might resent too much interference on his part. After all, wasn't there a fiancé somewhere?

'How are you getting along with the workers and their families?' he asked.

Her lips twisted. 'Not very well.' She told him of the reception of the African women in the compound. 'They seem to resent me, Steve. I honestly cannot think why.'

'You were warned, you know, Kylie. By Mr Beck. He knew the feelings of the local people, especially in this part of the country.'

She gazed at him with perplexity. 'But I was only trying to help—Steve, if you could only see the babies, the flies, the dust ...' She shuddered and Steve said, 'Anyone would have told you their reaction to your offers of help, if you had cared to ask. To them it isn't help but interference. I guess that's what bothers Saviko more than anything else. More than the fact that you've decided to come and live here, on the mine.'

50

He gazed at her profile as she turned her head, gazing out onto the sun-filled garden. She was frowning as he went on, 'No doubt he was hoping that after your father's death he would have the place to himself.'

He took another long pull at his beer. 'And speaking of the mine, now that you have had a chance to evaluate it, what do you think of your inheritance?'

'I—I like it very much.'

He threw back his head and laughed. 'Even with Saviko wishing you all kinds of evil? Come on, now, be sensible, Kylie. When are you letting Mr Carvalho wind up the business and going back to civilization?'

Her lips firmed. 'I'm not leaving at all, Steve. I told you. I'm staying.'

'For Pete's sake ...! You've had the chance to look the place over by now. Anyone can see its not worth very much ...'

'Is that why you're so intent on buying it?' she snapped, her eyes flashing.

He looked amused. 'What a contrary child she is, to be sure! I just want to help you. The mine is worth very little these days. Your father, you must know, had been battling. It's not worth very much to me, either, except that it borders my own land.'

'You're wasting your time!' she told him, eyes snapping angrily. 'In the short time I've been here I've become rather fond of the Sheila Mine.'

With a quick movement he stood up, facing her, his face tight. 'Don't you see what you're facing, you little fool? The danger, the loneliness ...?'

Kylie, too, rose to her feet, facing him, head held high and proud.

'No, Mr Jamison, I only see a place that my father dreamed about for twenty years, a dream that, through sheer perseverence and hard work, he made come true.'

There was a look in his eyes she couldn't put a finger to. A look that was still there when he left, changing gears noisily on the ancient Land Rover and speeding along the dusty driveway as though trying to escape his own anger.

During the night the rain came, thundering on the tin roof like the hooves of a thousand stallions. Kylie raised her head from her pillow and peered anxiously at the window, where the wildly blowing curtains told of the fierce wind that accompanied the rain. The top half of the old-fashioned window was wide open and throwing the blankets back she went over to close it. She woke to see a soaked garden, the lawns flooded, debris from the battered trees and bushes littering the muddy ground.

Mr Carvalho was already at breakfast when she appeared, finishing his third cup of coffee. 'Morning, Miss Graham. Did the storm disturb you?'

Nodding, she inspected the table, the fresh fruit and deliciously crisp bacon that Poppy had prepared. 'It did. Woke me up.' Seating herself opposite Mr Carvalho, she poured her coffee. 'I see what you mean by flooding rivers and ruined crops. Nothing, I should think, could survive that sort of rainstorm.'

A thought struck her. 'I've been meaning to ask you, Mr Carvalho. Where does Vito sleep? Is there someplace around here where he stays?'

'Your father built a cottage quite close to the mine workings. It's convenient for Vito to get to work. The cottage is usually occupied by the mine manager, but once Anna Marie joined me here, your father suggested we stay in the house and let Vito have the cottage to himself.'

Reaching across the table he buttered a piece of toast. 'You cannot see the cottage from here, of course, but I assure you it is quite comfortable. Vito seems to prefer

52

it. Much more privacy, you understand.'

Smiling, Kylie nodded. The good-looking young man might be grateful for that. With his looks, there must be a girl around, somewhere. Perhaps even staying at the cottage with him.

'Would you perhaps care to look over the books this morning?' Mr Carvalho said, rising from the table. 'It's such a terrible day. This would be an excellent opportunity.'

'Sounds like a good idea,' Kylie smiled. 'All right.'

They spent the next couple of hours pouring over the ledgers Mr Carvalho kept locked in the old-fashioned safe in the small study.

'This is the ledger in which records of all the stones we find are entered,' Mr Carvalho said. 'It details every find and the name and number of the worker who made the discovery.'

Later, rising, he placed the book back on the shelf in the safe and brought out a black tin box. Putting it on the desk before her, he said, 'These stones were only found a few days ago and we haven't had time to get them into the bank at Umbaya.' Smiling at her rapt expression, he spread a white cloth on the desk top and taking a black leather bag from the tin box, tipped a pile of rough looking stones onto the cloth.

They didn't much look like emeralds, Kylie thought, expecting to see the brilliant green glow that to her, of all the precious stones, was the most beautiful. Disappointed, she picked up one, a dull greenish stone with smooth edges but lacking the luminescence of the true emerald.

Seeing the crestfallen look on her face, Mr Carvalho laughed. 'Everyone acts that way when they first see the stones. They have to undergo a certain amount of cutting and polishing before they begin to look like the

53

emeralds the world knows.'

He frowned, picking up one and examing it critically. 'Really, Miss Graham, I'm a bit disappointed in our present output. We are coming across stones now that are far inferior to the ones your father first discovered . . .'

'Why is that?'

'Who knows? The vein running out, perhaps.' He shrugged. 'If there's nothing else you would like to inpect . . . ?' He left the question unfinished, looking at her.

Kylie shook her head, and stood up. Later that day she thought a lot about his words, and about Steve Jamison's offer to buy the mine. Perhaps, as Steve implied, she *was* being stubborn in insisting on keeping it. Paul's letter, the only one she had received since her arrival, had been vague in the extreme regarding his departure date to join her. 'Give it a little time, darling,' he'd written. He hadn't, she decided, seemed in the least eager to join her, or even *see* their proposed new home. She sighed, and went to find Poppy, wondering if she could help in the kitchen. Her own company, suddenly, had become very tedious.

SIX

The days went by in quiet pleasant simplicity and Kylie learned more and more about the mine, the people with whom she lived and the country.

Her interest in the house and garden had worked wonders. A spot of bright new paint here, gay loose covers for the settee and chairs in the lounge, some judicious weeding of the flower beds in the garden, discovering, to her constant delight and amazement, exotic plants and flowers that she had never before seen. She commandeered a couple of boys with swinging sickles to cut the grass and soon the place was looking fresh and attractive.

Vito came once or twice to see her, seeming to take his off duty hours now when before Mr Carvalho told her he hadn't bothered. More than once she wondered at the dark look Anna Marie gave her whenever she and the young Italian where together, a brooding stare that made the small chin lift in defiance, returning the dark glance with one of her own.

She had grown used to the heat. She felt a certain pride of ownership and if Paul didn't write as frequently as he should have done, she hardly even noticed. Although excited whenever one of his letters arrived, there was no desperate longing to see him again and she found herself wondering once again about her own feelings.

Several weeks went by and since that other night she had not heard the strange noises again. Tired, at the end of a busy day, however, she felt she could easily have slept through them. If, her common-sense told her, there had *been* noises. Had it, perhaps, been the heat? The strangeness of her surroundings? Imagination could play tricks at the best of times. How much more likely to do just that out here, with the dark brooding jungle all about her and a man like Saviko playing on her fears ... ?

Then one night she sat up late in bed, writing to Paul. Her conscience had bothered her and tonight she felt she just had to get that letter finished.

She had just finished it, placing the envelope on her bedside table and turning off the lamp, when the sounds came again. They were much like the other time, an insistent thud-thud, low voices chanting some weird hymn.

Quickly she turned the pressure lamp back on and slipping her legs from the bedclothes she got out of bed. Standing by the window she listened, trying to distinguish the source of the sounds. They seemed to come from the far side of the garden, from an ancient summer-house that was never used. Without thinking she got a flashlight and thrusting her feet into slippers, she drew her dressing gown about her and went outside.

Her bedroom had glass doors, like all the other rooms in the house, leading straight onto the verandah, and she made no sound as she walked swiftly across the wooden boards and down the steps to the garden. She ran the beam of the torch in front of her. The grass was damp below her feet, soaking through the thin soles of her slippers. The strange, insistent thudding of the drums was all about her, in her head as she walked.

It was as if it drew her towards it and she seemed to have no will of her own, her steps leading unerringly to the source of the sound. She put her hand on the rough wooden door of the summer-house, blistered with its years of tropical sunshine, ramshackle and almost lost in a tangle of vines and creepers.

And suddenly the door was swinging open under her hand. It was opening despite the fact that once before when, curious, she had tried to enter, to see if anything could be done to the old place, it had remained inexorably closed.

Inside the summer-house the thudding was loud, and yet as she stood there, holding her sudden terror in check, for she could feel cobwebs clinging to her face and hair, a soft scattering that told of other equally frightened creatures disturbed by her presence, she knew the drum was not there. There, but not there!

How perfectly ridiculous! she told herself. Kylie Graham, if there *is* someone using this summer-house for his own nefarious use, then its time someone stopped it, whoever it is. It was her property and she had to find out what.

She had lowered the flashlight, resting on the top of a worm eaten wooden box, when she realized it wasn't so worm eaten after all. On the contrary, the wood was new and black letters were stamped on its side. It seemed to be a packing case of some kind. She picked up the torch to examine it more closely, bending to feel with onehand, and froze as a sound came from behind her.

In the open doorway stood a figure, hooded and cloaked and from within the shadows of that garment peered a face so hideous that she felt her senses spin, saw the flash of a knife blade and for the first time in her life she fainted.

She woke to find herself laying on the bed in her own room. She was cold and shivered uncontrollably and Anna Marie, who leaned over her, a worried frown between her dark brows, turned to say something to someone behind. She heard Mr Carvalho's voice answer, 'Try and find out what happened. The poor girl's in shock. Do you think we should phone Umbaya for a doctor?'

Kylie closed her eyes as she heard Anna Marie say, 'I don't think so, papa. She'll be all right . . .'

Again from Kylie's view came another voice. 'I'll fetch

some brandy.'

This time she recognized the voice as Vito's and struggled to sit up. The entire household seemed to be there, including Poppy who peered from behind everyone else from a face grey with fear.

As Kylie moved the whole room spun and she sank back, murmuring, 'Oh . . . !'

A firm hand pushed her back onto the pillow. 'You are not to move.'

Anna Marie looked down at her and Kylie was amazed to see that her eyes held compassion. The corners of Kylie's mouth twitched. Not at all in character! she thought. Anna Marie, of all people . . .

She said, 'The—the thing had a knife! Did—did he hurt me?'

Once more to her surprise there was the sound of smothered laughter and Anna Marie answered, dryly, 'There is nothing wrong with you, Kylie. You fainted. Vito was coming to see my father about something and saw the beam of your torch on the porch of the summer-house. He investigated and found you laying there.'

'Gave me one hell of a shock, too, I can tell you.' The young man approached the bed and gazed down at Kylie's white face. 'Can you tell us what happened? What on earth were you doing out there at this time of night?'

He gave her a reproving frown. 'You were covered in dust and in the dark could quite easily have walked straight into the pool.'

Once again Kylie struggled to sit up, this time managing to suppress the waves of blackness that threatened to sweep over her. 'The man in the summer-house,' she breathed. 'The door was open . . .'

The group of people in the room exchanged glances. She saw Mr Carvalho shrug as he said, 'Open? Of course it wasn't open, Miss Graham. That place hasn't been used for years. Not, anyway, since your father bought the mine. It's falling to pieces.'

'But it was,' Kylie persisted. 'The door opened easily when I pushed it and inside there were wooden packing cases with letters on them . . .'

Anna Marie smiled faintly. 'You sure you didn't get a bump on the head too, as well as fainting?'

'I did *not* get a bump on the head too,' Kylie said, a little stiffly, and swung her feet to the floor. 'I want to see . . .'

'You'll do no such thing,' Mr Carvalho told her. He handed her a glass in which clear amber liquid glowed. 'Be a good girl and drink it up. It's brandy.' He turned to the others. 'Let Miss Graham get some sleep. In fact, all of us had better get some sleep. We'll all feel rotten in the morning.'

'There *were* packing cases,' Kylie said after the men had gone, leaving her alone with Anna Marie. 'And noises and a figure in a dark cloak. I wasn't mad or insane or anything, Anna Marie. I *did* hear those voices.'

'Shhhh . . .' The dark girl bent to tuck her in, suddenly attentive. Once again Kylie was amazed at how wrong she had been in judging the girl's character. The lovely Portuguese girl tonight seemed to be all concern.

It just didn't make sense. Like, Kylie thought, as she sunk back on the pillows, the drums and the frightening figures and the knife . . .

She felt the warm glow of the brandy making her sleepy and heard Anna Marie say softly, 'The noises will not come again. Not tonight, anyway.'

Kylie's eyes shot open. 'Then you *did* hear them?'

'I've heard them—not that they have ever tempted me to venture out into the darkness to see who or what was making them, but I have heard them.'

'Then why didn't you say so when the other's were here? They must be thinking me crazy . . .'

59

Anna Marie looked away. 'There are things it is better not to know about, Kylie. My father would tell you those sounds came from the workers compound. Noise carries a long way in this country.'

But, catching a glimpse of the dark eyes before Anna Marie turned out the light, Kylie knew she was lying.

Before breakfast the following morning, more to convince herself that she hadn't been dreaming than anything else, that the whole thing had actually happened, Kylie went to the summer-house. She pushed at the ancient door with all her might. It didn't budge. In fact, to her examining eyes, it appeared as though it hadn't been open for years. And yet Kylie knew it had! How *could* she have dreamed it . . . ?

Standing on tiptoes she tried to look into the window, but they were so encrusted with dust and the green mildew of age that it was impossible to see anything. So intent was she that the voice behind her made her stumble, and she felt a hand go out to steady her.

'I had the whole place swept out this morning. It was a disgrace. Should have been pulled down years ago.'

Mr Carvalho stood beside her, smiling. He said, 'How are you feeling this morning, Miss Graham?' Then without waiting for her answer, he said, eyes on the weatherworn hut, 'We really should do something about it. Don't you agree?'

After he'd gone Kylie lingered for a few minutes longer. She gazed down at the dusty wooden floor of the tiny porch, looking for footprints. But the only marks were those of a stiff broom, sweeping away any traces of these. Her own and the intruder's . . .

SEVEN

The following morning Kylie stood by the battered jeep that, apart from an ancient truck, seemed to be the Sheila Mine's only method of transport, and watched Vito work on the engine.

The day was very warm and the young Italian had removed his shirt, wearing only brief khaki shorts in the heat. His torso was muscular and very tanned and his teeth gleamed in his dark face as he smiled at Kylie. She stood near, admiring the deft hands as they probed inside the bonnet.

She laughed once, saying, 'You should have been a mechanic, Vito, instead of a book keeper. Just what made you, anyway? Become a book keeper, I mean?'

He shrugged, not looking at her, eyes busy on the greasy mess of the engine. 'My family thought I would make more money that way, I suppose. In our own country we were very poor, too many children. When I was old enough I saved enough money to emigrate and chose this place. I like the sun. Could not have lived in some country with grey skies and much rain.'

He straightened, wiping his hands on a piece of oily rag. 'I suppose it was much the same reason why your father came here, too, Miss Graham. To see what life held in store for him?' He gestured about them, taking in the dusty piece of garden where they stood, the columns of ants carrying away the tender young shoots of the flower seeds Kylie had planted a week ago. 'I often wondered what your father saw in this place, how he stood it, knowing he had a home and ready-made family waiting for him in England. And, now I have seen you, Miss Kylie,' grinning, his eyes frankly admiring as they rested on her sun-bleached hair and flushed cheeks, 'I wonder even more.'

'Vito!' They turned and saw Anna Marie coming towards them, eyes flashing, a sense of determination in her step that made Kylie smile. Seeing them together Kylie had sensed the possessiveness the girl emanated whenever Vito was near. Kylie guessed she had no intention of letting the handsome Vito out of her sight for a minute longer than she possibly could.

'Yes, Anna Marie?' His tone was patient, almost wary as he turned to meet her. Anna Marie's eyes rested on the bare chest and immediately flew to Kylie. 'My father wonders why you are not at the mine office.' Even though she spoke to him her eyes held Kylie's. 'There has been some trouble there and he sent a message that you must come at once.'

Vito sighed, and threw the oily rag into the jeep. 'I'll come at once, quirida caro. But first I must wash,' holding his hands out, 'see! It will take me but a few minutes.'

'All right, but hurry.' Anna Marie turned to retrace her steps. 'I'll tell the messenger.'

Vito's eyes followed her, then he looked at Kylie. 'She is a lovely woman, yes? my Anna Marie. But a very jealous and possessive woman also.'

Kylie laughed, for her supposition had been correct. Vito and Anna Marie were in love. And even if Vito was not as enamoured as Anna Marie, Kylie guessed he would find it difficult to escape ...

Reaching for his shirt, draped over the low branch of a tree nearby, he shrugged himself into it, looking at Kylie with frank curiosity. 'But what is it I hear about *your* beloved, Miss Kylie? That you have left him behind in England? No?'

At her shrug and hesitant, 'I thought it would be

62

better if I saw the place first. There was no hurry to get married.'

Again he glanced at her covertly, and added in a curious tone, 'You both were not dying to get married, then?'

'Dying to? Of course not.'

'If I loved someone who was going far away, I would not wait.'

'We have a lifetime ahead.'

'In the state of the world today, particularly this part of the world, who can tell? For me, were it possible, it would be marriage instantly. No waiting.'

Frowning, Kylie regarded him for a long moment in silence. 'You really mean that? That you couldn't wait?'

'If you were really in love, you would not want to.' He broke off, aghast. 'Forgive me, Miss Kylie. I did not mean to imply that you were not both in love . . . Mama mia! I *am* making a mess of this conversation, aren't I?' He grinned at her sheepishly and Kylie looked at him with sympathetic eyes. 'But you love Anna Marie, and yet you say you would marry instantly . . . ?'

'Her father objects.' Another, hopeless shrug. He seemed strangely embarrassed and Kylie said soothingly, 'Don't look so upset, Vito. It'll work out for all of us, I'm sure. And you haven't upset me, really.'

She stared after his retreating back. Vito's remarks had banished everything else from her mind. Gone was the memory of the dark, cloaked figure, Saviko, even the mine. Thoughtfully she recalled how several of their friends viewed with amazement her intention to come out here alone, for Paul to continue with his job in London and join her later.

'Don't you *want* to be married before you go?' they had asked, and Kylie had laughingly replied, 'why the hurry? It doesn't do to be too impulsive,' she told them.

63

'Just because you lot cannot wait, doesn't mean to say Paul and I are the same. Everyone's different.'

'I know,' they had murmured, 'but . . .'

Now, walking through the hot dusty morning Kylie wondered why the sudden doubt. She loved Paul and he loved her, so why should she be affected by Vito's unthinking declaration?—'if you were really in love, you would not want to wait . . .'

Did the fault lie with her? Did the hesitation about their marriage, the stubborness Paul loved to tease her about—really stem from the fact that she wasn't sure? Why, suddenly, her mind filled with doubts about her engagement to Paul?

As the day wore on the thought assailed her more and more. Each time she pushed it away, but Vito's words, 'If you were really in love . . .' circled her head like the words of some half-forgotten song that repeats itself over and over again.

And yet, she had to remind herself, it was really her fault. Hadn't Paul said they could get married right away, still go on that cruise? But she had been adamant, determined she would come out to the Sheila Mine, and, once here, equally determined she would stay. Thinking back she knew she should have felt eagerness, a delight in his suggestion. But she hadn't minded the wait, she thought, experiencing a sudden fear. *Were* they really in love? They had known each other such a short time before becoming engaged. But that didn't mean a thing. Lots of their friends got married within weeks of meeting—some, these days, didn't even bother, just moved in together.

Perhaps, she thought inconsistently, I should have had other affairs, perhaps then I should have been able to tell the true meaning of love, or just attraction. But Paul had been the most good-looking, the most charming man she had ever met. He had 'swept her off her feet', as her mother had so quaintly put it and his kisses had swept her into realms of longing.

Her fear increased. Somehow, thinking back, that feeling was no longer with her. She tried to visualize Paul's unruly hair and laughing brown eyes. Instead Steve Jamison's deeply bronzed features took its place and she felt herself go hot all over, Vito's unthinking words hammering afresh at her brain.

'Careful.' The warning broke into her thoughts, startling her and she turned to see the man who filled her thoughts approaching from the direction of the house. 'Anna Marie told me you were up here,' he said, and took her arm, pulling her away as he spoke from the thorn bush with its inch-long spikes into which, in her preoccupied state, she would have walked.

He grinned down into her eyes. 'Best not to tangle with those! They always win.'

She smiled, acutely aware of the hand that held her arm, lightly but firmly, just above the elbow. As though sensing her feelings, he released it and looked up at the hillside above them. 'Seen anything of Saviko since our last meeting?'

Kylie shook her head. 'No, and I don't particularly want to, either. The longer he stays away the better, as far as I'm concerned.' The happenings of the previous night intruded for a brief moment but she pushed them away, hearing Steve say, lightly, 'He's a harmless old boy, really.' His eyes teased, making her flush.

'Harmless!' Her own eyes snapped. 'I can't say I much care for your definition of harmless! He's an old—what's the male equivalent to a witch?—an old *goblin*.'

Steve laughed. 'I expect you're right. Anyway, do we have to spoil a perfectly lovely day talking about Saviko? Come with me. I've got something to show you.' Won-

65

dering what it could be, glancing at him from the corner of her eye, Kylie followed him. She noticed the carefully pressed slacks, the snowy white shirt, open at the throat, the sleeves turned back to reveal deeply tanned forearms, covered in fine black hairs. Usually he wore khaki, a safari suit with either long or short trousers. Today he looked different, as though he planned to visit someone special. She wondered who that someone could be and a pang went through her, imagining some girl, some neighbour, born to the country, golden tanned by the sunshine, watching for him from the verandah of a white farmhouse . . .

She caught her breath and looked away but her eyes retained the black hair shining with cleanness and good health, a thick lock resting over one eye where the wind had played faint havoc with it. Her eyes, as if of their own accord, moved back to his face. In profile it seemed more relaxed today, portraying a new tenderness unfamiliar to Kylie. She stumbled a little and brought her mind back to the difficult and stony path they followed. She thought she'd rather die than muff this outing, looking stupid in Steve's eyes. A woman on his hands was a complication, anyway. Pausing briefly, Steve looked back and inquired, sweetly, 'Having trouble?' Then, without more ado and before she could find breath to answer, he grasped her arm and practically dragged her over the path beside him.

'Where—where are we going?' she asked at last. 'How much further?'

'I admit its not exactly a walk for a lady of leisure, but I promise you'll enjoy it,' was all he would say, his smile faintly indulgent. When she didn't answer, he went on, 'Hasn't anyone told you that you happen to have rather important ruins on your property? Few tourists know about them or would even bother to come all this way, they *are* a bit inaccessible, but are nevertheless an important find, especially in the field of archaeology.'

When Kylie still didn't answer, too breathless to speak, he pointed upwards, to the summit of the hill and Kylie gazed upon the ruins of which he had spoken, a tumble of grey stones made smooth by the passing of centuries. Outlined against the brilliance of the sky, they stood in solitary splendour. Climbing the last few feet, Kylie collapsed with a grateful sigh upon the base of a broken column.

The ruins crowned the very summit of the hill, offering magnificent views of the plains and valleys below. Clothed with tawny lion-coloured grass, littered with grey rocks with bright lichens and the violet shadows made by the late afternoon sun, they were a fascinating sight. She wondered why no one had mentioned the ruins to her before. But that was one thing about Steve —he took far more interest in her 'education', as he would no doubt call it,—than anyone else. But there would be an ulterior motive behind that interest, that of softening her up for the final bid . . . And, she thought, if events like that of the previous night continued to happen, that might be a lot sooner than he anticipated!

She looked up at him, blowing out her cheeks in a parody of exhaustion.

'Phew, that was quite a climb! No wonder the ruins don't get many visitors! They would have to be crazy about archaeology to want to climb this far.'

'I told you it wasn't exactly a climb for a lady of leisure,' he told her, a hint of steel creeping into his voice. 'You would do far better to go back to London and sell the place to me.'

Kylie sat with her back to the ruins. Had she noticed that the sky had darkened, great clouds rolling up to obscure the sun, casting dark shadows over the ruins;

shadows of former terrors, she might well have kept silent. But as it was she was only conscious that once again Steve Jamison was trying to force her to sell.

'For a lady of leisure, perhaps,' she replied, eyes flashing, 'but I no longer consider myself that.' She rose from her porch on the broken column and walked over to the very edge of the hill, gazing downwards. 'I have to admit that you've been pretty decent in your interest in my welfare, but I'm sure you are only doing it out of a spirit of "noblesse oblige." In other words,' she turned to face him, cheeks flashing scarlet, 'beware the Greeks bearing gifts.'

Steve laughed. 'I'd hate to be on the wrong side of you, Kylie.' His voice held deep feeling. 'Man, could you hate!'

That shook Kylie a little. Her feelings were quite clear to her and she certainly didn't *hate* Steve Jamison. Her feelings about him were far too subtle for that. She was wary of him, suspicious, perhaps, she even disliked him at times, but hate—never!

She looked around her at the ruins and shivered, imagining the fearsome deeds that had perhaps been perpetrated in this ancient fortress of some great African Chief. 'Let's go back, Steve. I—I think it's creepy.'

His smile mocked. 'Don't tell me you're scared of a pile of tumbledown stones? A Women's Lib. type of girl like you, Kylie? Now *that* I refuse to believe.'

'Believe it or not, Steve, but I want to go back.'

On the climb down she disciplined herself against his nearness, although grateful for the steadying hand, feeling its warmth on her skin. They spoke little and yet as if by some magical process all restraint was removed and the silence grew friendly and companionable. The clouds built up, throwing long shadows across the hillside but as they reached the more gentle slopes the clouds moved temporarily from the sun, so that it seemed to shine through in a red and gold mist, lending an air of enchantment to the day. The limpid atmosphere would soon give way to approaching night. The long rays of the sun tipped the long grass with silver, seeming to cast a blush of tawny rose across Kylie's cheek, turning her eyes to a deep purple.

As they neared the house she could not repress the sigh of regret that escaped her, for, in spite of the climb, she had enjoyed it and wished now she hadn't been so hasty in asking Steve to take her back. By the house they paused, listening to the sleepy twitterings of the birds in the eaves of the old house, breathing in the intoxicating scent of moonflowers freshly watered by one of the boys. After a while Steve said, and she thrilled at the reluctance in his voice, 'Well, I guess I'd better be going. I had intended calling on someone but I fear I've left it too late now. The lady might not relish a call at this hour. Thank you for not whining and moaning about the rough climb, Kylie. You were a brick. Most girls shudder when they are asked to do something that entails a little exertion.'

Kylie flushed, raising one hand self-consciously to a stray lock of hair that clung to her cheek, endeavouring, without much success, to tuck it back into the low crignon.

Steve's hand stayed her. 'Why do you wear your hair like that? It's beautiful.'

Feeling the flush on her cheeks deepen and hating herself for it, she murmured, 'It's—it's very fine and soft. It's—I've discovered it's the only way I can keep it neat and tidy.'

His mouth twisted. 'Who wants to be particularly tidy in this place? Wear it loose, Kylie.' He paused for a long moment and the silence was heavy, becoming

69

almost unbearable until he said, 'Let me . . .'

'No!' Her voice held alarm and she made as though to push his hands away. Then, as his fingers, cool, almost impersonal, found and loosened the clips that held the crignon together, she breathed out a deep sigh and sat, stiffly erect, as the pale soft hair fell across her shoulders. His hands pulled strands of it forward, so that it fell over her bosom.

His voice was deep when he spoke. 'Your fiancé must be either blind or insane,' he said.

She felt, she was *sure*, he would kiss her. The air between them was so explosive. But he didn't, merely walked back to the Land Rover and climbed straight back in. With a brief, 'Goodnight, Kylie Graham,' he was gone.

The air was heavy with tension the next few days. Kylie woke from a troubled sleep at the slightest sound, the creaking of a bough in the wind, the scream of an animal disturbed in its nightly drinking place, the cry of a far-off hyena. But the other sounds didn't come again, and after a while she began to relax once more, to enjoy the brilliant sunshine and the cool green water of the swimming pool. Anna Marie seemed to want to make amends for her past coolness, and Vito visited the house more than Mr Carvalho cared for, hanging around whenever he could get away from the mine.

Steve arrived one morning with mail, saying he had been into Umbaya and it was no problem, anyway, taking the turn-off to the Sheila. There was a letter from Paul, and flushing under Steve's direct gaze, Kylie took it onto the verandah to read, accepting a drink from Vito as she did so.

Vito placed a tall glass of beer in Steve's hand, then vanished with Anna Marie in the direction of the swim-

70

ming pool.

Kylie read, then re-read the rather short letter, then folded it and placed it back in its envelope. When she didn't speak Steve raised dark brows, saying, larconically, 'Not bad news, I trust?'

Kylie flushed again, hating herself for being such a petticoat creature where he was concerned. Eyes gazing unseeingly at the brilliantly-lit garden outside, she shook her head. 'No, not bad news. Just—just unexpected.'

After a while Steve left and she sat alone on the verandah. She looked at Paul's letter again. He asked her to forgive him, but he had been on the arranged trip to the Aegean Islands—'I just couldn't stand it a minute longer, darling, you being away and everything. I drew the fare from our savings again—as you say, if the mine improves, we can always put it back! and treated myself to the cruise. I'm afraid my boss wasn't very enamoured with me and I'm once more on the unemployed list. But so what! Everyone asked me why I hadn't used the money to join you there, seeing I was sure to loose my job anyway. But you know, darling, I really don't think I can accept the idea of living so far from everyone we know and the life we are so used to. You say in your letters you've not been to a dance or a cinema, let alone out to dinner, in all the time you've been there! And although it doesn't seem to bother you, my sweet, I feel sure I would soon be climbing the walls living under those conditions.'

He went on to speak of a girl he had met on the cruise, 'the most gorgeous creature you could ever wish to meet. Her name's Guilia—of course, my sweet, not a patch on you, but she helped to while away the time very nicely. And you really cannot expect me to be a hermit while you are away now, can you? I wouldn't ask it of you in the same circumstances . . .'

71

Rising abruptly she went from the verandah, hearing voices coming from the direction of the swimming pool. She needed company, and a fast crawl across the fresh clean water, cleansing her of that feeling of distaste with which Paul's letter had left her. The idea seemed to act like a tonic, restoring her spirits to their usual jauntiness.

In her room she changed into a one-piece costume of lime green, tucked her hair up under the rubber cap and grabbing a large towel, for Poppy saw there was always a plentiful supply of these in the bathroom, she emerged into the sunshine. Already it was beginning to swelter as the day wore on. A twisted tree had collapsed during one of their recent storms and lay across one end of the pool, the long pointed leaves smelling of eucalyptus as they floated on the green water.

She stood on the rough concrete verge of the pool, her eyes tightly shut against the sun's heat, her arms outstretched in front of her and dived in. The water closed over her, icy, for a brief moment taking her breath away. Then she gave herself up to it in sheer delight. Half a dozen times she swam the pool's length, then, panting a little, swam to the side and hoisted herself up to sit with her slim golden tanned legs dangling in the water. She pulled off her rubber cap and the water which had been trapped inside splashed out, over her legs. Leaning back on her outstretched arms, she lifted her face to the sun. It was quiet and peaceful and deliberately she pushed all thoughts of Paul from her mind, telling herself she would not let it upset her. There would be time enough to decide what to do when she had made up her mind about the mine.

The letter had probably been written in a fit of remorse and knowing Paul, his changable ways, he would be sorry immediately he had posted it . . .

'My goodness! You are taking this seriously, aren't

72

you?'

It was Anna Marie's voice and Kylie wondered dreamily who she could be talking to. She had thought, after their swim, she and Vito had gone inside, for there was no sign of them near the pool area. Another voice answered, slowly, lazily. 'I'm taking it seriously because it *is* serious.' This time the voice was Vito's and Kylie opened her eyes with a snap. 'The police, if she should bring them into it, will check on Saviko and the cave, and, if they have any sense, the boys in the compound.'

Kylie could imagine the shrug, as he went on, 'But you know what they are! They will all swear they know nothing.'

Kylie sat very still. The fallen tree hid her effectively from the two people standing on the other side of a flowering shrub. For a moment she held her breath, trying to adjust her mind to the words she had just heard. Her teeth bit into her lower lip, refusing to believe it, refusing to acknowledge the fact that, a few yards away, Anna Marie and Vito were standing together, discussing the witchdoctor and the mine.

There was silence. Deliberately Kylie pushed herself upright, standing and picking up her towel from the ground. She heard Anna Marie's voice say, 'Don't you like me anymore, Vito? You've been—been different since *she* came.'

Kylie could imagine the pettish frown on the pretty face, the way the full red lips pouted, and her own lips tightened.

Vito's voice answered, tensely, 'You *know* how I feel about you. But I don't think we should be standing here like this, so openly. Supposing your father, or anyone else for that matter, should . . .'

'Pouff! You were not worried at one time, my Vito, about such things . . .'

73

c*

Anna Marie's voice died away and Kylie risked a peep around the large bush.

She saw how the girl put her arms about Vito's neck, pulling his dark head down to her own, kissing him. It was a slow lingering kiss. She heard Vito's deep chuckle, saw him gently disentangle Anna Marie's arms from about his neck then pat her luscious bottom before saying, admonishingly, 'Anna Marie! You're too much of a temptation for one man! Don't you know that?'

Perturbed at what she had heard, Kylie did not move until she heard their footsteps die away. Then she ran across the grass to the house, going in the back way and disturbing Poppy at her ironing. The African girl gazed after her, a knowledge in the dark eyes that would have disturbed Kylie even more had she seen.

EIGHT

In spite of her misgivings she slept well and after breakfast next morning, she was seized with a sudden desire to
face Vito, perhaps bringing the conversation around to
Saviko to watch the young man's expression as she spoke.
A thin white mist lay on the lower slopes of the hill.
Even so, the heat was scorching, an aggravating thing
as she started up the slope towards the mine. Then for
a moment a thought stayed her. What if she should run
into Saviko or any of his men?

Could she depend on herself to play the pioneer
woman facing danger in a new, wild country, surrounded
by unknown terrors and evil? After all, her home was
really in London. Maybe Paul had something when he
mentioned the wilds and being so far from all they knew
and expected?

Then with a sudden spurt of anger, she thought, 'For
heaven's sake, Kylie Graham, was this the spirit that saw
your father through all those lonely years? I doubt if he'd
have got far if he'd thought like you.'

With a determined step she began to climb, toiling
up the steep path at a pace that left her breathless. After
a while the muscles in her legs began to protest at the
unaccustomed exercise. She paused for a moment, blowing the hair from her eyes and gazed upward to where
Saviko's cave was. Was he, at this very moment, watching her? She suspected very little escaped his notice and
she guessed that whatever he could not keep track of
himself there would be eager acolytes to help.

'Idiot!' she told herself and resumed the climb. Once
through the belt of trees on the lower slopes she saw the
heavy ground mist had dispersed. She lifted her head to

75

see Mr Carvalho coming to meet her.

Giving her a searching look, he began, 'I wouldn't advise you to visit the compound this morning, Miss Graham. There has been a bit of trouble.'

'Trouble! What sort of trouble?'

'A couple of agitators. Oh, we get them on and off, making their rounds, stirring up trouble with the boys. They, of course, will grasp at any excuse to halt work for an hour or two.'

Kylie frowned. 'Then we should go to the police.'

'My dear young lady, do you realize just how far the nearest police station is? No, we have to deal with this our own way.'

Kylie's frown deepened. 'But why should they listen to agitators or want to strike?'

'Higher wages. Better conditions.' His tone was scornful. 'Who knows? They don't know themselves half the time.'

'I can't say I don't agree with them,' Kylie answered, thinking of the flies crawling into the babies eyes, the hot, dreary huts in which the mine workers and their families were forced to live. But common-sense told her they all looked well-fed and happy. The children especially. The fact that there was a definate lack of hygiene couldn't be blamed on the mine.

Mr Carvalho frowned. 'If we give in to them, Miss Graham, increase their wages and other benefits, you might just as well return to England, and sell the mine to Mr Jamison. As it is, we barely pay our way.'

His words didn't surprise her, really. He had warned her, hadn't he, about the state of their finances? Perhaps she *had* been too optimistic, too sure of herself and her capabilities.

'What do you want to do?' she said. 'You say we deal with this ourselves. How?'

'We have our ways.' Mr Carvalho regarded her with

a frown. 'Let me get Vito to take you back to the house . . .' His voice took on a different note. 'It's really no concern of yours . . .'

'It's every concern of mine,' Kylie answered him firmly. 'I want to see how you handle it.'

A sigh that spoke volumes. 'All right! If you insist. But don't come too close. Stay in the office with Vito. I don't want any unpleasantries, especially where you are concerned.'

She followed him to the office, where Vito stood in the open doorway, on the handsome face a look of dismay. Crowds of African men stood about, mostly in groups. Their dark eyes seemed to gravitate to the trio by the small office, their attitude wholly aggressive, their eyes wary, faces blank.

The mine manager walked towards them, slowly, purposefully, and they muttered among themselves, drawing closer together. There followed a lengthy discussion during which Kylie watched their expressions, trying to access the effect of Mr Carvalho's words on them.

Then a movement caught her eye and turning she saw the tall thin figure of an African man edging towards the entrance of the mine tunnel. Just before he faded into the dark entrance he seemed to hesitate, then turn, looking straight at Kylie, mouth agape in a derisive grin. It was as though she stood once more in the doorway of the summer-house, the hooded figure before her, the same derisive smile showing decayed teeth . . .

All sense of caution deserted her and she looked at Vito. 'Wouldn't you like to show me the mine workings while they're talking, Vito? I haven't seen any of them yet, you know.'

She smiled at the young man and obviously uneasy he hesitated. 'I don't think Mr Carvalho would like it,

Miss Kylie.'

'Don't let's tell him then. Just a little tour!' Her voice took on a weedling note and Vito capitulated. Darting a quick look at the mine manager, still haggling with the workers, and totally unaware of them, he murmured, 'All right, then. Only a short tour. But,' gazing doubtfully at her white shirt and jeans, 'you really should wear an overall and safety helmet.'

Kylie shrugged. 'These old things! It doesn't matter, Vito. They'll wash.'

'A safety helmet then,' Vito insisted.

Kylie nodded, her eyes on the entrance to the mine. 'If you say so.'

A few minutes later, the white helmet placed securely on her fair head, she followed him into the narrow opening of the mine. Suddenly it was dark. A complete blackness that filled her eyes and ears and seemed to blot out all sounds. The tunnel smelt mouldy, the only sound a constant drip-drip that must be water coming from lower down the tunnel. She told herself unwillingly that she had to see what the man was up to. Her feet found stones on the floor that she stumbled on, one hand going out to Vito for support. After a moment he lit the tiny torches attached to the front of their helmets and Kylie saw the dark empty tunnel narrowing away before them.

They appeared to be the only people in it. The workers, she supposed, would be all outside, arguing with Mr Carvalho. And yet, she *had* seen the tall man come in here. There was nowhere else he *could* go but down this tunnel. Why? Why the tunnel? The question ran round and round her mind like a caged squirrel. There was no answer that seemed at all likely.

For a long moment they stood watching, listening. There was nothing and uneasily at last Vito said, in a low voice, as though frightened, 'There is nothing to see, Miss Kylie. Please let me take you back. Mr Carvalho

78

will be most upset if he finds you have been down here without his permission.'

'Upset?' In the semi-darkness Kylie turned to face him. 'Why should he be upset?'

A shrug of the shoulders. 'No one is allowed down the mine but himself and the workers. No one. I myself have been down only once before. Mr Carvalho will be very angry ...'

Kylie made an impatient movement. 'You've already told me that.'

Thoughts raced through her mind. Uneasy thoughts that she shrugged away. She turned, making her way further along the tunnel.

'Miss Kylie!' Vito called after her and began to follow, stumbling over the rough surface. 'Please come back.'

The plaintive note in his voice made her hesitate, briefly, then she ran on. That man was up to something. Probably a thief! Then a thought struck her and she paused, allowing Vito to catch up. 'I am going down this tunnel,' she told him firmly. 'I saw a man go down here and I want to know exactly what he is up to. If you're so scared of what Mr Carvalho might say, go back and tell him what I've told you. About the man. Say I saw him enter the tunnel and I'm certain he's up to no good. Also you can tell him that I'm sure its the same man who was in the summer-house.'

She saw him blink in bewilderment and gave him a gentle push. 'I'll wait here until you get back.'

Stubbornly he shook his head. 'Mr Carvalho would kill me! I could not possibly leave you here alone.'

Exasperation overtook her. Suddenly she was the Kylie telling her mother and Paul that she *wouldn't* sell the mine, on no account. That she would continue with her father's dream, come what may.

'Then wait there,' she said, and turning began to run

79

lightly along the narrow stone passage, leaving the young Italian gaping behind. The tunnel began to veer to the right and soon she could see nothing of Vito's light. The one on her own helmet flickered, becoming weaker by the minute and she wished she'd asked him to swop headgear before she left him.

A narrow gauge railway line ran down the centre of the tunnel, making walking even more difficult and after a moment or two she had to slow her pace, for it would be easy to twist an ankle on the iron rails. Once or twice she had to resist the temptation to turn and run, let Mr Carvalho handle the trespasser. The hot dusty air all about was the air of tombs . . .

'Honestly, Kylie Graham,' she told herself. 'Your imagination! Tombs indeed!' Mr Carvalho should be here any minute, accompanied by Vito. She waited, her ears straining for the sound of footsteps. Then through the vacuum of silence came a sound like far off thunder and at the same moment the light on her helmet went out. 'Damn,' she muttered beneath her breath and removed the headgear, shaking it, peering at the tiny light to see if it would come back on. She had no idea how it worked—batteries, she supposed. Why did Vito have to give her a dud one? Now that darkness was complete she felt fear begin to stir, a fear that emerged in a scream as the sound of rumbling drew rapidly nearer, and a dark shadow came rushing towards her.

It was no more than four or five paces away when she realized what it was. The shadow gave way to substance and she saw a large iron skip, a trolley on wheels used for removing the loose earth and stones from lower down the tunnel, heading straight for her.

Then a wave of hot anger passed over her and she cursed herself for having fallen into such an obvious trap. For being so stupid. She had refused to listen to Vito, making it easy for anyone to catch her helpless.

The rumble of the skip reverberated along the tunnel. She closed her eyes and pressed her body against the tunnel face, holding her breath until bright lights flashed behind her closed eyelids. Any minute now she would be slammed against the tunnel wall. She felt the rush of air as the heavy skip rolled past. Then she began to shake and it was only with an almighty effort that she was able to control herself. The whole world began spinning and she knew that if unconsciousness drifted over her she was lost.

But for the moment the danger was past. With a bit of luck she should be able to make her way back along the tunnel to blessed daylight. Providing, as a sudden horrible thought struck her, no one was waiting quietly in the darkness further along the tunnel . . .

Tentatively she took one cautious step, when she heard a faint rattling. A shifting of stones under someone's foot. Removing the heavy helmet, she held it firmly in one hand, then began to tiptoe back along the tunnel. It would make an excellent weapon and now that her eyes had become accustomed to the darkness she found she could see much better, spades and tools that had been left laying about that she hadn't noticed on her way down.

She wondered if she would be capable of using violence if it became necessary. Then, thinking of the way the heavy skip had come hurtling past, she knew she was. Her fingers curled round the rim of the helmet, securing a good, firm hold. She waited. The footsteps drew nearer. Then stopped. A voice called out, 'Miss Graham? Are you all right?'

Letting out a sigh of relief Kylie stepped into the spotlight of the torch Mr Carvalho carried. 'Yes, I'm all right,' she told him.

'You gave me a terrible shock,' he accused, sternly, frowning at her. 'Why did you do such a foolish thing?

81

Vito told me you were babbling all sorts of nonsense . . .'
His mouth tightened. 'I'll see that he loses his job over
this.'

Kylie was shaking her head. 'No, Mr Carvalho. It
wasn't Vito's fault. I insisted on going down the mine
tunnel. He was very much against it.'

'But why on earth . . . ?' Obviously the mine manager
was lost for words. 'Such a foolish thing,' he muttered
again. 'So—so insane. Dangerous, too.'

'It was that all right,' Kylie agreed, wryly.

By now they were once more out in the bright sunlight. He noticed for the first time that her hands were
grazed from where she had been flung against the rough
face of the tunnel. 'But you are hurt!' he said accusingly.
'Come into the office. I keep a first aid box there. We'll
see if there are any deep cuts.'

Seated on the chair in the small office, Kylie endured
patiently the mine manager's ministrations, watching
him closely as he worked with gauze and plaster. Had he
known about the man in the tunnel she wondered? Had
that been the reason for Vito's nervousness and Mr Carvalho's anxiety? She shivered. She had never been so
aware of her aloneness as she was at that moment.

Poppy peered anxiously at her as Mr Carvalho
escorted her back to the house, calling for the African
girl as they neared the verandah. Later, as Kylie emerged from the bathroom wrapped in a large towel, the
maid hurried in with a tray of tea. Her dark eyes rested
on the dressings on Kylie's hands and her face puckered
as though she was about to burst into tears. Knowing
how very warm-hearted the girl was, Kylie forced a
smile. 'I'm all right. Really I am, Poppy,' she said reassuringly.

'No! No! Madam, you are not!' Poppy's voice rose in
protest. 'Better you leave this place.'

'Don't be ridiculous,' Kylie said. 'You don't really

believe in that old man's ravings, do you?' For without putting it into words she knew the girl suspected Saviko of being responsible for her injuries. 'In any case,' she smiled, holding up her bandaged hands, 'Saviko had nothing to do with these. I—I fell in the mine tunnel.' A thought struck her. Supposing the man in the tunnel had been in Saviko's employ? The witchdoctor wanted her out of this country. In a place like this there would be hundreds of ways to carry out his bidding. Especially when he had discovered that trying to frighten her away —thinking of the night in the summer-house and the strange, frightening sounds—hadn't worked.

The girl rolled her eyes. 'There are reasons for everything, madam. Everything he says. It may take much time but it will happen . . . You do not understand the powers of such a one as Saviko.'

She saw that the girl was almost grey-faced with terror, that her ample body shook with fright as she spoke the witchdoctor's name. This old man certainly knew how to put the fear of God into these simple people, Kylie thought. Anger took the place of the weariness she had experienced a few minutes before. 'There is nothing to fear, Poppy,' she told the frightened girl. 'Boss Jamison has spoken to Saviko and he says the old man talks with much wind. That his words are empty. You must not be afraid of him. Do you understand me?'

The girl nodded and bent to pick up the towel Kylie had dropped to the floor. Kylie reached for the cotton kaftan of lime green patterned with flowers of white and dark green, and slipped it over her head. Wonderfully cool after grubby tight jeans she had just discarded. She went to sit in front of the dressing table and lifting her hair brush began to sweep it through her long hair, finding it so difficult with her bandaged hands that Poppy said, shyly, 'Let me, madam.'

Kylie watched her through the mirror but, intent on

her task, the girl avoided her eyes. Later, folding the discarded towel and holding it to her breast, she said, softly, 'The madam needs anything else?'

'No, thank you, Poppy. Thanks for the help.'

Kylie watched her leave the room. Obviously she knew something. But Saviko held these people in the grip of such fear that she would never tell Kylie what she knew. Even, wondered Kylie, if it became a matter of life and death? She pushed her hair back from her forehead. It was useless to try and guess how they would act in any emergency.

She felt dreadfully tired now and her hands hurt. She lay down on her bed, trying to relax on the rather lumpy mattress and thought of Paul's last letter, of the strange noises that came in the night, of the wooden crates in the summer-house that were there and then not there. And more than anything else, the puzzling behaviour of Anna Marie, one minute the carefully cultivated insolence, the next a strange compassion that the dark eyes could not hide.

NINE

Everyone was preoccupied at dinner and even Anna Marie seemed to be affected by the general atmosphere of unrest. Mr Carvalho finished his meal quickly and left the table and later when Poppy had placed the coffee tray on the verandah Anna Marie said, almost negligently, 'My father tells me you had a little mishap at the mine this morning! It was a very foolish thing to do, to enter the mine tunnel alone.'

'I wasn't alone.' Kylie didn't try to disguise the teasing note in her voice. 'Vito was with me.'

She caught Anna Marie's swift dart of suspicion and went on smoothly, 'At first, anyway.'

The dark girl's lips tightened. 'My father tells me you sent Vito away and went on alone.' Curiosity was plain in her eyes. 'What could you have hoped to see? There is nothing but dust and rock . . .' She shuddered. 'I have been down once only. I would certainly not wish to go again.'

Kylie lifted the small coffee cup to her lips, watching the other girl over its rim. She would, she decided, say nothing of the events inside the tunnel. The terrifying moment when the skip came rushing towards her. Not until she was very sure of her ground. And then only to Steve . . .

The piercing cry of some large bird wakened her at dawn, its 'Kreek-kreek' breaking the deep silence of the morning. Kylie lay there, gradually awakening. The events of the previous day seemed like a dream. Could it possibly have happened? That someone had tried to kill her? She raised herself on one elbow and poured the

85

tea Poppy had placed on the bedside table.

It was only then she noticed the slip of paper tucked under the saucer. Unfolding the note, she saw Steve's handwriting sprawled across the page. 'Kylie—I shall be over later today. Care to go visiting? Regards, Steve.'

When he came for her, driving the Land Rover and looking very handsome and debonair in white slacks and shirt, he leaned over to help her in, then drove away with hardly a pause. 'There's someone I want you to meet,' he said, almost abruptly. 'A very dear friend of mine.'

Kylie thought of the girl he had mentioned once before and she wondered, momentarily, why he should want them to meet. Perhaps because they would be neighbours one day, she thought, when the girl and Steve were married. If, and the thought shook her, she, Kylie Graham, was still there!

The idea was so disconcerting that tears rushed to her eyes. Idiot! she told herself. But the day had lost its glow and the sun felt unaccountably chill on her shoulders. They drove without speaking for most of the way, along the usual rutted track, then turned off along a still narrower track, the jungle-like undergrowth on each side rasping the sides of the vehicle as Steve sent it shuddering past.

Finally Kylie could see where the thickly wooded country ended and they emerged into an open space where a rather overgrown garden surrounded a small house. Rather, she thought, like her own at the Sheila Mine. The thatched roof was grey with age, looking as though a mere spark would send it up in flames. A long verandah ran the length of the house in front and as Steve brought the Land Rover to a standstill, Kylie saw a white-clad African appear and come down the steps to meet them.

'Boss Steve!' he breathed, dark face lighting up with delight. 'Miss Eve will be so glad to see you. Come in, do. I'll make some tea. And we have some English biscuits. Or,' smiling shyly at Steve, 'would you prefer some beer?'

'A beer, Jeramiah, if you don't mind. Although I'm sure Miss Graham would love a cup of tea.'

'Will be with you in one moment.' The old servant vanished and Steve, holding her lightly under the elbow, escorted Kylie up the flight of shallow steps and through the screen door.

'You'll love Eve Nash,' he said. 'She's the most incredible person, Kylie. Just what this country needs. Tough, uncomplaining, but with a gentleness and femininity that makes her the most beautiful woman I've ever met.'

He grinned at her, eyes teasing. 'Present company excepted, of course.'

Kylie joined in his laughter. 'Of course!' But her heart sunk. She didn't *want* to meet the most beautiful woman Steve Jamison had ever met! She didn't want to see the way his eyes shone whenever he spoke of her.

She said, 'We mustn't stay too long, Steve. I . . .'

But he wasn't listening. His eyes were fixed on her hands, as though noticing for the first time the white bandages. 'What on earth did you do to your hands, child?'

He took one in his, gently, and run one thumb over its palm, blue eyes searching her face for an answer.

Kylie felt herself blush under that intense scrutiny and turned her head away. 'I—I . . .'

At that moment a woman appeared from the direction of the glass doors further along the verandah. Her face lit up at sight of the tall dark man rising to his feet at her approach. 'Steve! How perfectly lovely to see you! It's been simply ages.'

Kylie turned—and gasped. The woman hobbled along with the aid of a stick. Her hair curled about her head in crisp white curls. Her skin was pink and white and the eyes, although faded to a pale shade of blue, took in every aspect of Kylie's appearance in one swift glance. Steve went forward to meet her, assisting her into a straight-backed chair that she indicated with her stick. 'That one, Steve. I would never get up from one of those,' laughing towards the sagging but extremely comfortable chair where Kylie sat.

Immediately Kylie, too, was on her feet, smiling uncertainly at the elderly woman. She glanced at Steve for guidance, and he, after settling the woman comfortably in her chair, said, 'This is Kylie Graham, Eve. Her father owned the Sheila. Remember?'

'I remember. How do you do, Kylie Graham? How do you like our country?'

'And this, Kylie,' Steve went on, smoothly, smiling at them both, 'is Mrs Eve Nash, my very dear friend.'

Kylie smiled, feeling suddenly very shy and awkward. 'How do you do, Mrs Nash? I love the country.'

The woman gave her a sharp glance. 'Steve tells me you refuse to part with your land. You intend to stay, then?'

Kylie nodded. 'I intend to stay, Mrs Nash. Definately.'

The conversation turned to other things, Mrs Nash adroitly by-passing any further talk of the Sheila Mine or Kylie's refusal to sell. She said, after a short pause during which the servant brought Steve a fresh beer, 'I believe, too, Kylie—you don't mind if I call you Kylie, do you?—I knew Tom Kylie well, as well as I knew your father, and liked them both, I believe you have already had a clash with old Saviko?'

When Kylie nodded, Mrs Nash turned to Steve.

'Don't you think it's time someone paid a visit to that old rascal and told him a few home truths? He terrorizes the local boys and their families to such an extent it's getting more and more difficult to obtain decent help. I haven't had a gardener for weeks. They are just not interested in working anymore.'

After that the old lady took charge of the conversation and more than once Steve caught Kylie's glance, his mouth twisting humourously, as though to say, 'Humour her, Kylie. She doesn't have many visitors.'

Later, as they drove away, Mrs Nash's plea that they come again, and soon, ringing in their ears, Steve said, 'I've known her for as long as I can remember. She went to school with my grandmother, believe it or not. The Nash's were one of the first families to pioneer these parts, and Eve, at the tender age of six, came up in a covered wagon all the way from Pretoria. Took them four months. She's a grand old girl and I try to keep in touch as much as I can.'

They came onto the main road once more and Steve increased the speed of the Land Rover, sending it rocketing over the bumps and corrugations so that Kylie was thrown against him over and over again.

She said, after one particularly hectic stretch, 'Where are we going?'

'Before I take you back I want to show you where I live.'

Excitement took hold of her, making her eyes sparkle. 'Lovely. I often wondered where you lived and in what sort of a house.' She giggled. 'I bet it doesn't look in the least like mine.'

His mouth twisted at one corner. 'Not in the least.' He turned his head to look deep into her eyes and she felt the excitement turning to trepidation. An involuntary shiver went through her. 'As long as we're not—not

89

too late, Steve . . .'

His smile turned into a frown. 'There you go again! I'm taking you to my place and you are jolly well going to like it.'

It was an order, not a suggestion. Immediately her back was up. 'Oh! Who says so?'

He smiled down into her eyes. 'I say so, and I'm a lot bigger than you are.'

She found herself laughing, and leaned back in the leather seat, enjoying the day to the full. They were passing through a deep rift in the mountains and presently Steve craned his head back, directing his gaze upwards. 'I live up there.'

Kylie gasped, following his gaze. A white house perched like a goat on a ledge of rock, seeming to cling to the very mountainside. 'For heaven's sake!' she breathed. 'However did you manage to build? It looks an impossible task.'

'My grandfather built it. I told you, we've been here a long time. For that reason I don't want strangers taking over property on my very doorstep.'

'And that's why you want to buy my land?' Kylie gazed at him wide-eyed. Then her mouth twitched. 'Aren't I a stranger?'

Without answering he brought the Land Rover to a halt, pulling in to one side of the road, and turned to face her. Suddenly apprehensive, for they had not seen a soul, black or white, for miles, and the place seemed strangely desolate, Kylie found herself backing away, sliding along the seat as far as she could go without falling out. Why, she wondered, his sudden change of mood?

As though reading her thoughts Steve laughed, lifting both hands in mock surrender. 'Wrong! My intentions, I assure you, are strictly honourable. I want to show you

90

my domain, or at least, part of it.'

Kylie gave a shaky laugh, feeling foolish at her show of nerves and listened while Steve told her something of the history of the place. It was delightful among the hills. High in the clear sky a couple of hawks circled and dipped, looking for food, their wings outstretched and motionless in the clear air. Higher up, in the deeper clefts of the rocks, lilac and blue shadows merged with the dark greens of the fir trees that grew there, clinging as precariously as Steve's house. All among these hills, Steve told her, were gold reefs and small mines, all pegged out with notice boards.

Nearby stood the wattle and daub houses of the miners, deserted now, but still standing, as though waiting for the return of their owners.

'What happened to them?' Kylie was fascinated, listening to Steve, his deep voice expressing clearly the love he felt for this land.

He shrugged at her question. 'The veins ran out, or they became impatient. A lot of them couldn't stand the loneliness. Then there was fever and marauding animals. All sorts of things, Kylie.'

Much later when they were settled in comfortable chairs on the balcony of Steve's house, he concentrated his gaze on Kylie until she was forced to turn her head away, unaware that the heightened flush intensified her radiant appeal.

With those blue eyes on her she couldn't think clearly. She only knew that Steve, sitting opposite her across the white wrought-iron table on which a servant had placed a tray of drinks, had only to reach out for her and she would not hesitate. Paul might never have been, for the feelings she had for Paul were nothing to match the pang that went through her each time. Steve's hand accidently touched her's.

91

They sipped their drinks and gazed out across the valley, spread below like some giant landscape painting. The balcony afforded the most magnificent views. Through the glass doors leading to the balcony, the huge lounge was cool and dim, cooled by whirring fans. On the highly polished floor one magnificent leopard skin sprawled. The furniture was of a rich looking red-wood, highly polished and gleaming in the light from the large windows. A copper bowl filled with orange and yellow marigolds and green fern stood in the centre of a long coffee table before comfortable looking settees.

On the off-white walls hand-carved African masks hung, their empty eye-sockets brooding over the man and girl who sat so companionably together, reminding Kylie somehow of Saviko.

She looked down at her bandaged hands, then up, catching Steve's eye.

'You never did,' he said, 'tell me how you hurt your hands.'

She took a deep breath, and suddenly it was all pouring out; the strange nightly noises, the summer-house and the hooded man with the knife, the run-a-way skip in the tunnel.

Steve sat quietly listening, knees crossed negligently, one hand holding his glass. When Kylie had finished, ending on what, to Steve, sounded almighty like a sob, he frowned and leaning forward placed his glass carefully on the table, taking his time, his mind trying to sort out the facts of what Kylie had just said. 'Are you sure about this?' he asked, finally, looking up and catching her eyes.

Kylie nodded. 'Of course I'm sure! You don't think I'm making it up, for heaven's sake?'

'Of course I don't think you're making it up, Kylie. Only it,—well, let's face it, it sounds awfully far-fetched . . .' Seeing the way her face flamed, the soft full lips tightening, he grinned, wryly, adding, 'All right! All right! I wasn't doubting your word. But haven't you spoken to Mr Carvalho about it? Surely he must know what's going on?'

'I asked both Mr Carvalho and Anna Marie about the noises. They said they had heard nothing, that, because I was new to the country, it was probably all my imagination.' She looked at him pleadingly. 'It wasn't, Steve. Not my imagination. That night in the summer-house, when I saw the man and the packing cases, I *know*, I just *know*, that Anna Marie had also heard the noises, but she won't admit it.'

'And why do you suppose she won't?' Steve grinned. 'Especially if what you say is true and she *has* heard them?'

'It—it must be something to do with her father. Oh, I don't know!' She frowned. 'I'm sure, though, Saviko has something to do with it, Steve. All that mumbo-jumbo about my father's death and the pantomime telling me about myself and some man, lost in heaven only know's what place, and the danger that surrounds us.' She broke off, seeing the amused look on his face.

'Saviko tries to frighten everyone. You mustn't let him see he has succeeded with you,' Steve said easily.

Feeling more than a little hysterical, Kylie gave way to sheer fury. '*Frighten*? You're darn right he frightens me! Wouldn't you be scared, seeing one of those heavy skips, or whatever they call the things, rushing towards you and knowing there's no escape . . . ? Besides all the other things . . .'

He stood up abruptly. 'I'll go up and have another talk with the old boy, if that'll make you feel any better.' His tone was so casual that Kylie flushed even pinker. Rising, too, she said sharply, 'Perhaps you'd better take me home. I don't much fancy being on these roads after dark.'

'Of course.' Holding open the glass door, he followed her into the large airy lounge. 'What do you think of my home? You didn't say,' he smiled, calling a truce.

She looked around her at the lovely room, elegant but with a lived-in look that appealed to her greatly. 'I love it, Steve. It's beautiful. Did you . . .' she shot a sideways glance from her blue eyes, 'did you do all the interior decorating yourself?'

He laughed. 'If you're trying to inveigle me into admitting a female accomplice, you are in for a nasty shock. I did it all myself.'

'It's lovely,' she repeated.

'I happen to have such a diabolical temper that I would never ask any woman to share it with me. Or, if she did, she would have to go into it with her eyes wide open. Actually,' his mouth twisted, 'I've never yet met a girl and after knowing her for a little while thought I could live with her for ever. One day, perhaps, a girl will come along who will mean so much that I won't mind throwing away the freedom to go and do exactly what I like. That would mean bringing someone else into my private world. Perhaps, as I grow older, I sometimes doubt if there is such a girl for me. I'll probably grow into a crusty old batchelor who finds himself increasingly intolerant and less charitable as time passes.'

Not quite knowing what to answer, Kylie gave an uncertain smile and reached for the silken scarf she used for her hair. 'Thanks, Steve. It's been a perfect day. Thank you for allowing me to meet Mrs Nash. She really is a super person. I'd like to know her better. Perhaps I'll borrow the mine truck and drive over one afternoon.'

'Eve would enjoy that. Give her a ring first, to make sure she's at home. For all her years, she still is a very active woman. Belongs to various clubs and Women's

Institutes and does all sorts of welfare work, especially for the African women and children.'

Side by side they stood by the huge picture window in the lounge, gazing down at the valley spread below. The sun had began its descent and Kylie knew it would soon be dark. She moved uneasily, for he seemed strangely reluctant to make a move towards the Land Rover waiting in the driveway in front. As she moved, her bare arm touched his and it was though a magnet had drawn her towards him. His arms went around her, his eyes, so blue! so intense! gazed down into her's. She tried to twist her head to one side, to avoid those scarching eyes, but he raised one hand and holding her firmly but gently by the small chin his lips came down on her's.

The kiss seemed to go on forever, his other hand slipping up beneath her loose shirt, and finding the bare skin. She wanted to object, but she could not. Instead she gave herself up to the kiss, feeling his heart hammering against her's. This kiss was balm to her bruised spirit. In any case, this man, she knew, wouldn't let go no matter how much she might object. She realized he was a man who would brook very little interference in anything he wanted to do, and he obviously wanted to kiss her. And she didn't care! She was more than happy to kiss him back, to thrust the memory of the fickle Paul even further from her thoughts.

'Hmmm, you taste nice,' he murmured at last, lifting his head to laugh down at her. One eyebrow rose in that quizzical way he had. 'You didn't mind, did you? I believe in kissing my women thoroughly and often.'

Kylie smiled. 'Am I your woman?'

'You could be, in spite of all the nonsense I spoke about freedom and my private world.' Then, so suddenly it shocked her, he let her go, turning away to gaze once more across the darkening valley. When next he turned to look at her the warm glow that had overwhelmed her faded and she saw his expression was mildly contemptuous. 'But I forget. There's a fiancé waiting somewhere. I guess we both forgot.' He began to descend the rough grey granite steps that led to the driveway and walked to the Land Rover, waiting for her there, his back turned towards her. Bewildered, Kylie followed numbly, her cheeks scarlet. She joined him and climbed into the Land Rover, her back stiff with pride as she sat straight on the scruffed leather seat.

What must he have thought of her? Of course, he wasn't to know about Paul! Should she tell him? Explain the reason for her behaviour? Then the stubborness that was such an integral part of her nature came to the fore and she sat even straighter, lifting the small chin in a strangely endearing way. So thought the man sitting by her side, eyes fixed unwaveringly on the road ahead but still intensely aware of her every movement.

He came to a halt outside the verandah of the dark house. There was no sign of Mr Carvalho or Anna Marie and the place had only a small light burning above the steps that led to the screen door.

They sat for a few minutes in silence. Then Steve turned to her and said, 'I'm sorry about the kiss. It was just a kiss, a way of saying thank you for being so decorative and such pleasant company.'

Kylie took a deep breath, determined to answer him lightly, to show that it had meant as little to her as it had, apparently, to him. 'You don't have to worry that I'll take you seriously,' she said, forcing a laugh. 'I know you have your reputation to consider.'

His mouth twisted. '*My* reputation?'

'Yes. All that freedom stuff and having to live with one girl for ever. I could see it wasn't exactly your idea of heaven.'

96

Steve's only answer was to start up the engine and crash the gears in such a noisy manner that Kylie gasped, one hand going out to touch his arm.

'Don't! Everyone seems to be asleep.'

'In that case, you'd better join them.' They gazed at each other in the semi-darkness, the anger between them a tangible thing. 'I'd hate to wake anyone up.' His voice was sarcastic and her cheeks flamed.

'There is no need to use that tone of voice,' she said, hotly. 'Just because ...'

'I'll use any tone of voice I like with you, young lady,' he retorted. 'I'm not one of your employees, you know. Neither am I the man you so blithely left at home, with instructions to follow at your bidding.'

'I—I told you all about that,' she said in a throbbing voice.

'So you did!' he encouraged her. 'But tell me some more about this lover of yours. I see him as tall, handsome and very self-assured. Probably enjoys the easy life if he let you come all this way on your own. In fact, not in the least masterful ...'

'He doesn't have to be. I should *loathe* a man who bossed me ...'

'That, my sweet, is evident!'

Kylie blushed. 'He's fun to be with,' she said irrelevantly.

'Life doesn't consist of just having fun. I suppose he lets you have all your own way, and that's exactly what you like.'

'N—no,' she said faintly.

'No to letting you have all your own way or no to liking it?'

'No to me liking it. I'm *not* a child. I don't throw a tantrum whenever something happens that I don't agree with.'

D

'Poor Kylie! He really does sound like a cold fish, regardless of you saying he's fun. I wonder if he really is! I wonder if you even *know* the meaning of the word fun.' His smile mocked her. 'I wonder, too, if his kisses made your heart beat faster as did mine.'

She lifted her chin, refusing to answer. Of course they had, she told herself crossly. His very presence had sent her into a seventh heaven. Being apart from Paul had been unbearable. And yet, had it? She had hardly given him a second thought all these weeks she had been at the mine. Oh, of course, at first she had, longing for his letters, disappointed because they had been so brief and noncommittal. But the novelty of the mine had soon taken priority in her thoughts and thinking back now, their planned cruise to Greece, the spring wedding, had all been a pleasant dream . . .

As though reading her thoughts, he said in that infuriating way, 'I'd like to make a bet that you don't even know the difference between love and infatuation.'

'And you, from your vast experience, do, I suppose.'

'Experience is a very good word,' he murmured. 'Which you, in the field of love, seem to be sadly lacking. *If* you imagine you're still in love with a man who stays safely and comfortably at home while you brave the wilds of Africa in the raw.'

'It wasn't like that at all . . .' she began furiously.

'Don't shout,' he reproved her. 'You'll wake the household.'

'I'm not shouting,' Kylie said in a more moderate tone. She saw the hills behind the house were completely black by now, the bushes in the garden deep shadowy things that were strangely unnerving. 'I'm going to bed. Goodnight, Mr Jamison. Thank you once more for a *most* interesting day.'

She ascended the steps to the verandah, then hesitated,

98

to turn back to face him. He had alighted from the Land Rover and stood below her, his face on a level with her's. 'Why, do you suppose, do we always end up by fighting?' she smiled.

'I wonder? Do you think it could have anything to do with the love/hate relationship that every woman and man is conscious of but will not always admit to?' His eyes twinkled with suppressed laughter.

Kylie made a helpless gesture of protest. 'There you go again, making fun of me.'

Before she could stop him, he leaned forward and kissed her full on the mouth, holding that kiss for a brief, wonderful moment. Then he put his hands on her shoulders and gave her a gentle push. 'Go on. Go to bed. It's way past bedtime for little girls.'

Little girls! Kylie snorted down her nostrils disparagingly but before she could think of a suitable answer, Steve had gone, revving the Land Rover noisily as he rounded the bend of the drive and was lost to sight in the darkness.

TEN

'What do you think can be wrong with her?'

'I don't know. All I know is that she hasn't come to work this morning, which is unusual for Poppy. She's never done such a thing before.'

Kylie paused in the passage leading to the dining-room, hearing the voices of Mr Carvalho and his daughter, then entered, as Anna Marie said, disparagingly, 'They are all the same, papa. Don't you know that by now? Any excuse to take a day off work.'

But Kylie saw Mr Carvalho was shaking his head, a worried frown on his brow. 'I don't think so, Anna Marie. Not Poppy. She was with Mr Graham a long time, since she was in her early teens. No, I'm sure there must be some thing wrong.'

Kylie looked at the unset breakfast table, the room littered with last evening's coffee cups and exclaimed, 'Is Poppy sick?'

'That we don't know, Miss Graham.' Mr Carvalho gathered together the spilling ashtrays and handed them to his daughter. Anna Marie looked shaken for a moment, then, catching her father's eye, took them from him, her nose wrinkling at the stale smell of cigarette ends. 'She's always here. In fact, I cannot remember the last time she was off work. I'd better go and see if any of the garden boys have seen her.'

Silently, Kylie helped the other girl tidy the room, skimming the ever present film of dust from the tables and sideboard, plumping up cushions on the settees, re-moving faded flowers from the copper bowl of orange and yellow day lilies. Then she said, looking at Anna

Marie, 'What about breakfast? Shall I start?'

A shrug. 'If you are feeling so energetic! I'm not really very hungry.'

'Then fruit and maybe an omelette will do, and I'll put the coffee percolater on to boil. If we're not hungry I'm sure your father will be.'

But Mr Carvalho, when he returned, looked so concerned that Kylie's plans for cooking breakfast were forgotten. His face beneath that deep tan was pale and worried and to Kylie's question he shook his head. 'No one seems to have seen her. Not since last evening, anyway. Apparently she went to her room after she had finished here and after a few of her usual jokes with the rest of the staff retired to her bed. They all say they haven't heard a sound from her this morning.'

'But you looked in, didn't you?' Kylie asked. 'Wasn't there any signs of her leaving, or anything?'

'Nothing. The bed was neatly made. There was no way of telling if she had slept there or not.' The frown grew deeper. 'It really isn't like Poppy at all. Not in the least.'

Anna Marie laughed. 'Maybe she's eloped! Or had an assignation with a boyfriend and hasn't returned. After all, papa, we know very little of her private life, do we? I've always thought she was just a little too good to be true.'

Mr Carvalho frowned at his daughter. 'Don't joke, Anna Marie. I think I ought to inform the police, don't you, Miss Graham?'

Anna Marie made an impatient sound, her full mouth twisting in disgust, but Kylie said, nodding, 'I do. Get on to them straight away. Heaven only knows where the poor girl has got to, or what trouble she may be involved in. Definately phone the police, Mr Carvalho.'

After a hasty breakfast, and while she washed up the

101

few dishes, Kylie let her thoughts run back to the various occasions when Poppy had expressed fear whenever Saviko's name had been mentioned. The last time, particularly, after the incident at the mine tunnel.

She remembered Poppy, grey-faced with terror—'You do not understand the powers of such a one as Saviko.' Her voice rising to a wail. 'Better, Miss Kylie, you leave this place . . .'

'I managed to get through, although the lines, as usual, are bad this morning.' Mr Carvalho stood in the kitchen doorway, looking at her. Kylie, hands deep in the warm soapy water, turned to face him. 'What did they say?'

'Well, it's difficult . . . There isn't much they can do, Miss Graham. As they explained, Poppy could be anywhere. Perhaps taken into her mind to go off for a day or two.'

Kylie stared at him. 'But you said yourself Poppy was not like that! Surely she wouldn't just go, without telling anyone?'

'These people have quite a different set of values to us, my dear. If they decide they want to go home, back to their village, they go. The mere fact of informing their employer wouldn't even enter their heads.'

At Kylie's look of indignation—she hated it when he called them, 'these people'—instinctively defending the African maid to whom she had taken such liking, the manager went on, 'Now don't jump to conclusions. Poppy was no better and no worse than any of them. But she was still one of their people. If, say, she had received a letter, a message of some kind, that her parents were ill, or one had died, she would go without giving you, or any of us, a second thought.'

When Kylie didn't reply, he smiled and said, gently, 'I know how you felt about her, my dear, but not to worry. I'll ask the garden boys if they can find us a re-placement until she returns, for I'm sure she'll come back, just as though nothing had happened.'

Wishing that she had his faith, Kylie dried the few dishes, shining up the handles of the silver cutlery and placed them in the drawer. One last glance to make sure she hadn't forgotten anything—the teacloths washed and hung to dry on their makeshift line above the sink, the red geranium in its plastic pot that Poppy took such de-light in watered—and she was finished. Anna Marie had left the bedrooms tidied, the beds made, the windows open to the hot day. Now, feeling too restless to stay in-side the house, Kylie got the wide-brimmed hat she had taken to wearing and which had been made for her by one of the garden boys, the soft cream bark from some reed woven into intricate patterns and made into the shape of a sun hat, she went out into the garden.

A strange feeling of apprehension hung over every-thing. The gardeners bent over their tasks as always but with backward glances as Kylie passed. It was as though the war of nerves that Saviko had been waging all this time had come to a head and his macabre game had at last taken effect.

She paused to speak to one of the boys, a youth of about sixteen, weeding beneath the shade of a huge flamboyant. He cowered back, staring at her with wide fear-filled eyes as she remarked on the good job he was doing.

Her temper bubbled over. 'That's it!' she thought. 'Someone is going to have to do something about that man and if no one else is interested, then I'll do it. When the police come I'll tell them I want him removed. Saviko has frightened my boys long enough.'

The thought seemed to console her and, her mind made up, she began the climb up the hill. The mine compound was silent, the women sitting under the trees talking in low voices, the picaninies pausing in their games to watch her as she walked by. This morning there were no shy smiles, no sign of recognition as there had been of late, and for which she had been grateful, thinking she had finally captured their trust. Even if it had been given half-heartedly . . .

Of the men workers there was no sign. Even the little corrugated hut where Vito worked was quiet; hot and airless and darkly empty. Her hesitation, as she passed the compound and began the final climb to the cave where Saviko lived, was brief. She craned her head back, looking upwards through the scarlet msasas and told herself, grimly, Kylie Graham, you are going up to that old man and you are going to tell him that, unless he leaves your workers alone, the police will be the next to visit him. Not Steve Jamison or me, but the proper authorities.'

Of course, a small voice said, you should have done that long ago. Why on earth didn't you? After all, you cannot *know* he is responsible for Poppy's disappearance, can you? Hadn't Mr Carvalho said it could be anything? A death in the family? Sickness? And, by family, Mr Carvalho had explained, didn't necessarily mean immediate family. 'The whole village where they are born and spend their early years are, in theory, all family.'

So that could explain it! And yet—the thought nagged her like an aching tooth—Poppy would surely have come and told her, explaining why she had to leave.

Once again her thoughts went backwards—to the afternoon of the main tunnel episode. She pondered again the odd behaviour of the girl and her own thoughts that, should it become a matter of life and death, Poppy would ever admit to knowing anything. She recalled how she had deliberated on the matter, deciding finally it was

104

useless to try and guess how the girl would act in an emergency. And, was this, in fact, an emergency? Had Poppy been frightened off, before she could warn someone . . . ?

She paused to catch her breath, pushing the soft tendrils of hair more securely under the hat brim. Below her was the wide valley, furred with trees, vividly green where the river twisted and where they grew thick on its banks. The gorgeous shades of the msasas were fading now, turning to green and Kylie felt a strange sadness creep over her, erasing for the moment all thoughts of Saviko and the dark cave to which she was headed. She wondered if she would ever again see the glorious shades of pinks and reds and oranges.

Suddenly, on a clear patch of grass far below her, she saw a sable antelope. He was pale shiny brown in the sunlight, his magnificent outspread horns seeming too heavy for his head. He paused in his grazing for a moment to look up at her, casually, then carried on across the grass, the smooth muscled movement breathtaking in its unhurriedness.

A voice behind her said, 'Magnificent, isn't he?' and turning she saw Vito.

'I didn't hear you coming,' she murmured, wondering how he had arrived without her seeing him. He must have come from above her, from the hill crest, for it would have been impossible for anyone to have arrived unheard or unseen from below.

'I saw *you* coming, Miss Kylie,' he smiled. 'I was up there,' pointing to the thick belt of trees that merged with the deep blue of the sky.

Kylie wondered would he possibly could have been doing, but as he was obviously off duty she thought it no business of her's and repeated, feeling slightly foolish, 'I didn't see you.'

105

He laughed. 'No, you didn't. You were so deep in thought I was a little worried whether you would bump into the antelope or not.'

Kylie added her laughter to his. 'I wasn't *that* deep in thought! He looks harmless and is a truly magnificent creature, but even so I wouldn't want to approach too closely.'

'Where were you going, anyway? Isn't it a bit hot for a walk? And all on your own, too!' She saw he was looking at her curiously and laughed again, trying to make it sound light and flippant. 'I'd got some crazy notion about going up to see Saviko, confront him with the news that if he didn't get off my property I would call the police . . .'

He frowned, deep distress in the dark eyes. 'Has he been troubling you again, Miss Kylie? I understood he had been behaving quite well. I know for a certainty he has not been near the mine compound, for over a month. Not since Mr Jamison threatened him with the authorities.'

Kylie shrugged. 'Perhaps you're right, Vito. Perhaps I was a little hasty.'

'Certainly foolish, if nothing else,' Vito told her and took her arm, preparing to assist her back to the path.

Suddenly, the whole thing was ridiculous. Herself, going alone to see a man as feared as Saviko! She recalled the dark frightening figure in its black and no doubt filthy blanket and shuddered. Just as well Vito had arrived when he had. She must have been mad to think of such a thing.

Vito's voice broke into her thoughts. 'Why,' he asked, 'should you want to see Saviko anyway? Has something happened?'

'Yes.' Kylie bit her lip, wondering if he would think her completely mad when she said, 'Poppy is missing.'

106

'Missing?' Was there amusement in his voice, in the dark eyes, swiftly hidden behind a smooth exterior?

'Well, at least she didn't come to work this morning. Mr Carvalho seems to think she's gone off to her village.'

He nodded. 'I expect that's it. These people do, you know. It happens all the time. One of their more infuriating habits.'

'But surely . . .' Kylie was not going to be put off with soft words and smooth excuses. She'd had enough of that from Mr Carvalho. 'Surely she wouldn't just *go*? I mean, she must have had time to pack and prepare for the journey?'

As they spoke they had come half way down the hillside, reaching a part that she didn't remember seeing before. Huge rocks balanced precariously one atop the other, seeming to have been placed there by some giant hand and looking up Kylie could see where overhangs of granite-like stone made dark shadows above them. On this side of the hill there were few trees; instead of the glorious scarlets of the msasas there was only rough grey stone and the huge boulders . . .

'Play-things of the Gods,' Vito said, making her jump.

'Of the—what?' she murmured, gazing wide-eyed about her.

'That's what the local people call them,' he smiled. 'The play-things of the Gods. Human sacrifices were thrown from those rocks above,' looking upwards. 'It was, and still is, considered sacred ground.'

Kylie shuddered. 'The part Saviko didn't want my father to mine on?' she said, her voice a question.

Vito nodded. 'Yes, I'm afraid so, Miss Kylie. There was quite a fight between your father and the old witch-doctor, just before your father and Mr Kylie . . . well, just befor the accident.

'In fact,' he went on, taking her arm once more and

107

leading her down towards the path to the house, 'I'm never really comfortable walking on this side of the hill. Let's get away . . .'

They hurried past the pile of boulders, Kylie peering nervously in the long grass for snakes, for Mr Carvalho had warned her more than once of the danger of snakes in such locations—'They love the warmth of the rocks, and when the sun is hot will emerge from the crevices, basking in the long grass. One has to be extra careful in such places and step carefully.'

Perhaps it was because she was so preoccupied that they saw the figure in its blue and white print dress too late to avoid it. The dark curls were outlined against the grey stones and Kylie gave a scream as she almost stepped on one of the hands, outflung in the dust.

Poppy was lying, face down, her arms outstretched, at the base of a rock. She didn't move, didn't lift her head as Kylie screamed. She seemed so utterly relaxed and limp, her plump body resting as though the climb had tired her. But somehow her attitude was all wrong. A feeling of utter horror overtook Kylie as she gazed down at her. She heard herself say, 'Poppy?' and her voice held wonder as well as horror.

And then her forboding took definate shape. She saw, as one sees in a dream, the curious unnatural angle of the head, the small cloud of black flies that buzzed with terrible intention about the head. Knew, in that moment, that Poppy had not lain there herself but had been thrown there by someone.

Then Vito was beside her, kneeling, touching the base of the maid's throat. She heard her own voice, a frightened whisper, 'What . . . ?'

Vito looked up at her. He said, 'Miss Kylie, I—I think she's dead.'

It was one of those moments when time stands still.

With an odd feeling of reality, Kylie heard herself say, 'She must have fallen . . .'

She looked upwards at the rocks above them. 'From up there . . .'

Vito's answer came slowly. 'I don't think so. I think she was thrown.'

There was a long silence during which the only sounds where the shrill voiced birds in the msasas and the rising wind in the long yellow grass all about them. Then in a low agonized whisper, Kylie said, 'But why, Vito? Why should anyone want to . . . ? She *must* have fallen.'

Vito shook his head, not knowing quite what to answer. She heard him draw in his breath, heard the quiet control in his voice as he said, 'Whoever did it might still be hanging around. I don't think we'd better waste too much time, Miss Kylie, but get back to the house and report this.'

'We'll have to phone the police,' she murmured, and shivered. Her imagination pictured the dark satanic figure of Saviko, for she was positive it was he responsible for Poppy's death, lurking about in the trees, or peering at them from above, the sharp filed teeth bared in a grimace.

ELEVEN

That night was the hottest since she had arrived at the mine. Long after dinner, Kylie sat on the verandah, unwilling to even think of trying to go to bed. The only light came from the study window, where Mr Carvalho sat at his desk, busy with the eternal paper work.

Anna Marie came and joined her, throwing herself into the low cane chair with unusual violence, a sulky look on her pretty face.

Kylie gazed at her with sympathy. 'Why don't you go to bed?' she suggested. 'It's been a terrible day.'

The dark eyes met her's, hostile again.

'Why should I? Are you going?'

'Well, I will eventually. I don't think I could sleep just yet, however. I'd like to sit here awhile, until I get sleepy.'

A high whining noise made her lift one hand, brushing away the mosquito from where it had settled on her neck.

Anna Marie gave a short laugh, seeing the look of disgust that passed over Kylie's face as blood smeared from the crushed body. 'You'll get eaten alive! The mosquitoes are bad this year, after the heavy rains. You would be far more comfortable in your room.'

'Oh!' Kylie gave her a keen look. 'You wouldn't be trying to get rid of me, would you?'

Another laugh. 'If you do not object to playing—what is it you English call it?—playing gooseberry. Vito will be joining me in a moment.'

Immediately Kylie rose, brushing down the full cotton coolness of her thin kaftan. 'Sorry, Anna Marie. I didn't realize.' She looked at the girl in the darkness of the verandah. 'You love him very much, don't you?'

The girl nodded. 'I do. I think, without a life with Vito to look forward to, I would die. That is all that keeps me here in this terrible place, the knowledge that one day we will marry.'

Knowing Mr Carvalho's aversion to his daughter's romance with the good-looking young Italian, Kylie wondered. She said, 'And if your father should not relent?'

The girl glanced up swiftly, a question in her dark eyes. 'Why should not my father relent? What do you know about our affairs, anyway?'

Kylie hesitated, wondering if she should disclose the facts Vito had revealed to her, that morning as he worked on the truck. The morning that began her own doubts about her love for Paul.

She said, slowly, 'Very little, Anna Marie. Only what I have gathered from looking at the two of you together. You hardly bother, anymore, to conceal what you feel about Vito, and the way he looks at you would have many a girl swooning.'

'What is this swooning you talk about?' The girl frowned, head on one side. 'I do not like you to be impertinent where Vito is concerned.'

Kylie laughed. 'Swooning, my dear, means—oh, it's a pretty old-fashioned term. It could mean being powerless against his charms. Defenseless where such a man is concerned.'

Anna Marie shifted in her chair like a hen ruffling up its feathers.

'Please do not use words that I do not understand, then, Miss Graham.'

Kylie turned to go into the house, smiling, and at that moment there was the roar of a car engine. The bright

111

headlights blinded her as they swung round below the verandah, stones skidding beneath the screaming tyres as it made a swift turn, then came to a halt. Anna Marie rose from her chair, an exclamation of dismay on her lips, while Kylie froze where she stood.

A dark figure leaped from the car, far too dark to see what make or who the figure might be, only that it was a man. His arm came up and over, like a bowler at cricket, and the next moment Kylie saw a flame shoot up, terrifying against the night sky.

Anna Marie's scream rung out. Kylie heard the engine start up once more and the roaring of the flames. Then, as suddenly as it had appeared, the vehicle had gone, disappearing down the driveway and into the thick belt of trees fringing the main road.

Behind them, Mr Carvalho said, 'For God's sake, what happened?'

'A man in a car ...' Kylie began, and her voice was barely strong enough to be heard. 'The car stopped outside the verandah, down there, and the man in it threw something.'

With one accord they gazed over to the far side of the lawn where flames rose in red fury, crackling and hissing in the still night air.

'It's the summer-house, isn't it?' Kylie said, wonderingly. She gazed at the mine manager with wide eyes. 'Why on earth should anyone want to set fire to the summer-house?'

'I don't know.' The man's answer was curt. 'But if we don't do something about it, it could spread to the house. A spark ... This place is so old and dry, it would take very little to set it off, too.'

He strode to the screen door, opening it and shouting to the small gathering of garden boys that had appeared. 'Get the hose-pipe. Buckets of water. Use the swimming pool, it's easier than coming into the kitchen. *Get that fire out.*'

It was well past midnight before the last flame was extinguished. They stood on the lawn, the remains of the summer-house charred pieces of wood at their feet. A few thin spirals of grey smoke rose upwards, an errant flame hissing as it touched soaking wood then died down to a weak ember.

Kylie said, 'It doesn't make sense. Why on earth should anyone want to burn down that old summer-house?'

Mr Carvalho shrugged. His reaction to almost anything, Kylie was fast discovering. 'As you say, it doesn't make sense.' He looked up and met her eyes. 'Something else we'll have to tell the police when they arrive.'

But Kylie hardly listened to him. Her thoughts had flown back to the night she had followed the sounds to that summer-house, seeing the packing cases there, the dark hooded figure that had so frightened her.

Had somebody deliberately set fire to the place, thus obliterating all traces of the hut's nefarious usage? Or, more terrifying still, had the person who had thrown the grenade, or whatever it was, proved merely a poor bowler, and it had really been meant for the house? The verandah with them on it? Kylie felt a shudder go through her and Mr Carvalho, standing by her side, noticed and said, sympathy in his voice, 'You're all in, Kylie. Why don't you and Anna Marie make yourselves some hot milk and go to bed. There's little we can do here until the police come.'

Kylie nodded, grateful for his suggestion and followed Anna Marie into the house. She watched Mr Carvalho close the screen door behind them and wished it was something a little more substantial that stood between them and the night—perhaps even more bomb throwing. The door was designed to keep out mosquitoes and other annoying insects. Certainly not people of the calibre with which Saviko was now surrounding himself.

For she was positive the bomb had come from him—that the evil man who crouched in his cave on the hillside was even now conjuring up heaven only knows what other heinous ways to get rid of her.

The police didn't arrive until the following afternoon, and then only after Mr Carvalho had telephoned for the third time. The wires, it seemed, were once more in order but it was anyone's guess for how long. The thin copper was a great temptation for the natives who lived around here, invaluable as bracelets and ankle decoration, as well as numerous other things.

Kylie stayed purposefully in her room while Poppy's body, wrapped in a blanket and looking strangely small and vulnerable, was loaded into the back of the police vehicle. Not at all like the plump and usually cheerful girl Kylie had come to like and respect. She cried in her room, head on crossed arms, until Mr Carvalho, watching with his daughter from the verandah as they loaded the body, called to say the police wanted to speak to her.

Kylie sat, still and white-faced, signs of the recent tears still in her over-bright eyes, and described how she and Vito had found the maid. She couldn't help but notice the sharp glance from Anna Marie as she said this, or when the young constable mentioned he would also like to talk to Vito.

Hesitantly, Kylie said, 'He—he really doesn't know any more than me. We were—we were together when we found the—the body.'

The young khaki-clad policeman smiled, enjoying, for once the more tedious part of his job, that of questioning the people involved in the crime. This pretty girl with her blonde hair and wide blue eyes and crisp decisive way of answering his questions, was a welcome change

114

from the usual vague characters who were never quite sure of what they had, or had not, seen.

'If you don't mind,' he smiled, 'I'd still like to talk to the young man.'

Later, he stood with Mr Carvalho and Kylie, looking down at the sorry mess of the summer-house. 'And you say the car was being driven too fast for you to see who the man was? Whether he was a European or an African?'

He looked at Mr Carvalho who nodded. 'I didn't see it, but both Miss Graham and my daughter did, and they are both quite positive about that. It stopped for a brief moment, the man threw the grenade, and then it was gone.'

The policeman's mouth pursed thoughtfully. 'A pretty skilful piece of driving for one of our local boys, if, as Miss Graham insists, old Saviko had anything to do with it.' His eyes rested thoughtfully on Kylie's face.

She had told him about the incident in the mine tunnel, and the sounds that had led her to the summer-house and the hooded man with the knife, and although he had looked a little concerned, especially when she'd mentioned the run-away skip, she had noticed how the young police constable's eyes had met Mr Carvalho's and the condescending grin they had exchanged.

As though, she thought, resentfully, they laughed at her!

The policeman asked, 'Your first time in Africa, Miss Graham?'

She nodded and Mr Carvalho murmured, 'Miss Graham is, I'm afraid, inclined to be over-imaginative.' The police officer's grin widened and Kylie thought she would like to scream as the mine manager added, dryly, 'But aren't we all when we first come to this country?'

Trying to make out, she thought heatedly, that I

115

dreamed the lot!

But not, looking down at the ruined summer-house, the grenade and Poppy's murder. These even Mr Carvalho could not pass over as dreams or imagination.

The police officer despatched two of his African constables to question Saviko while he accepted Mr Carvalho's offer of cold beer. It was almost dark before the men returned, laughing and joking, as though they had been on a picnic instead of investigating a murder. She watched the young policeman's expression as his two men told him of their hunt for the old witchdoctor. He didn't, thought Kylie, seem to be particularly concerned when they said the old man had not been seen for weeks. Did Saviko's evil influence extend even to the African police? she wondered.

Seeing Kylie's watchful expression, the young policeman told her, 'No one has seen Saviko for weeks. I'm afraid, Miss Graham, unless we have definite evidence, there really is no way of implicating him in the—ah, various episodes you mention. Of course, the African woman's death is another matter. Rest assured we'll do everything in our power to find out what happened.'

'But you don't really think it's murder, do you?' Kylie's tone was icy. 'In that case, there isn't much use you wasting your time here, is there? There must be hundreds of far more simple cases for you to investigate.'

'Kylie!' Mr Carvalho's voice held a reprimand. 'The police cannot do the impossible . . .'

She was aware that the man had began to address her by her first name, a fact that ordinarily would not have bothered her. In fact, she would have welcomed it. Now, angry at the way the two men were treating her, she turned towards him, eyes flashing. 'I don't expect the impossible! I *do* expect someone to take me seriously, though, and not quite so blatantly show they take the old

116

man's word against mine . . .'

The policeman frowned. 'I'm sorry if I gave you that impression, Miss Graham. I knew your father well and admired him tremendously. He looked upon Saviko as a kind of joke, someone who kept the mine boys in hand when they got out of line.'

'That wasn't quite the way I heard it,' Kylie flashed. Her mind went back to Saviko's pantomime outside his cave, the very real fear it inspired in her as the witch-doctor painted the picture of death in the waters of the swollen river. Her father's and Tom Kylie's . . .

It seemed another life when she'd first heard his name, old Mr Beck saying, 'Saviko's a law unto himself . . . It would be better not to antagonize him, Miss Graham.'

And then another picture came into her mind. A man and a woman, in some desolate place, danger between them and safety . . . Saviko's second premonition. She felt her spirits lift, for this time Saviko would be proved wrong. The man had to be Paul, and Paul would not be joining her—not any more.

Steve came the following morning. The lovely hot weather continued. Mr Carvalho and Vito went about their work as though nothing had ever happened. Kylie marvelled at their coolness.

She was in the garden when Steve drove up. Sitting behind him in the Land Rover was a figure curled up into a ball as though to ward off a blow.

Steve brought the Land Rover to a halt and climbed down, yanking out the figure by the shirt collar. Kylie straightened from the wide bed where she had been sewing flower seeds—something that kept her mind effectively off the terrible happening of two days ago.

She frowned, shading her eyes from the bright sunlight with one grimy hand, looking at the frightened man Steve held by the collar.

117

Before she could speak, Steve grinned, saying, 'Look what I brought you!'

'Steve!' She glared at him, quick sympathy showing in her eyes for the cowering man. 'What are you supposed to be doing?' Then, before he could answer, 'Don't you know what's been happening here? It's been awful ...'

He nodded. 'I heard. This chap,' giving the unfortunate African a shake, as a dog would a rat, 'is an encyclopedia of information. Fortunately he had been imbiding in the local brew that passes for beer, a potent stuff that had him out cold within thirty minutes, and so one of my men who heard him bragging was able to persuade him to come with him to answer some questions.'

He turned towards the man and gave him another shake. 'Now, my friend, talk! Tell the madam all you know concerning the Sheila Mine and old Saviko.'

At the mention of the witchdoctor's name the man cowered still further, seeming to huddle inside the ragged khaki shorts and shirt that passed for clothing.

'What can he know?' Kylie cried, feeling sorry for the man. 'Oh, don't, Steve,' as Steve gave him another shake, making the man's eyes roll back in his head, showing the whites.

'He knows one hell of a lot. He happens to be one of Saviko's regiment of helpers. He's not nearly as scared, either, as he makes out. One moment's relaxation on my part, and he'd be off like a rabbit. I took the precaution of divesting him of his armoury, though,' reaching into the Land Rover to produce a broad, wicked looking knife that had Kylie shuddering. 'So he's lost some of his sting, if not all. Don't be fooled by his looks, Kylie. Believe me, he's still as unpredictable as a snake and just as vicious.'

Once more he turned to the man. 'Now, I'm going to

118

ask you once more, my friend, and this time I want some answers. Or perhaps you would rather Saviko heard about your co-operation with the police force?'

The man's eyes, red-rimmed, blinked. 'I have co-operated with no white police force, you know that . . .'

Steve's mouth twitched. 'I know it, but Saviko doesn't. Is he going to believe you when he hears you have been seen driving with the white man in his car? Or when my boys tell the villagers that you were seen going into the police station in Umbaya? That, too, I can arrange.'

'He will know I have not done this of my own free will.'

'Will he?' Steve grinned into the man's frightened eyes. 'I wouldn't count on that, my friend.'

Blackmail! thought Kylie. Sheer, unadulterated black-mail! She looked at Steve in a new light, seeing under the smooth pleasant exterior the tough pioneering spirit that had seen his forefathers through all the hardships, the infamous years when the country was being slowly wrestled from the dark ages and brought into the twentieth century.

Suddenly the man broke into a gibberish Kylie could not understand. He stopped as suddenly as he had started and Steve released him, causing him to sag against the body of the Land Rover. 'Thank you, my friend. You don't know how grateful I am for that information. Now get out of here. And,' grinning into the man's face, 'if you have any notions about running to Saviko to warn him that you have been forced to betray him . . .' Steve made a cutting gesture across his throat with one finger, '. . . if he does not kill you, I will.'

The man stood upright, then began to run, stumbling along the dusty driveway to the road.

Steve watched him go, chuckling, then turned towards Kylie. 'Don't look so shocked! The plan worked, and

119

that's really all that matters. It doesn't matter how you get there, as long as you do.'

'What did he tell you?' Kylie gazed at him wide-eyed with shock. 'He seemed so frightened. Absolutely terrified.'

'As well he might. Saviko will skin him alive if he ever finds out.' He grinned down into her eyes. 'We're not dealing with nice, polite people now Kylie, my sweet, but some of the most unsavoury characters this side of Cape Town.'

As always, when he called her, 'Kylie, my sweet,' she felt herself flushing, and lowered her eyes from the intent gaze of his. Why must he always make her feel so ineffectual—so gauche . . . ?

She said, 'But I still don't understand! Unless that man knows something about—about Poppy's death, I don't see how he can help? And you haven't told me yet what he told you . . .'

Ignoring her questions, Steve took her hand and turning it palm upwards in his own large brown hand, said, frowningly, 'Have you been doing some gardening? Shame! Look at the blisters already popping up.'

To her utter confusion he raised her hand to his mouth, kissing the earth-stained palm. He held it there for so long that Kylie felt her heart begin to hammer, knowing, blast him! that he read her thoughts in her eyes.

Withdrawing it swiftly, she turned away. 'Oh, Steve, be serious! I'm determined to do *some*thing. Even if I have to demand that the police arrest Saviko and take him into custody . . .'

'As soon as the word got to the old boy, he'd disappear,' Steve said. 'You wouldn't see him for dust. There is no better place in which to hide than these mountains and Saviko knows them like the back of his hand.'

'I'd still like to see him deprived of his freedom,' Kylie said, her voice grim.

'You and a few other people, Kylie. The police have longed for years to pin something on the old devil but he's always been too cunning for them. In any event, if Saviko knew you were really intent on bringing the police to him, he might do you some harm. He wouldn't be above that, blaming it on an accident. Then he could put miles between himself and this place. The police might never catch up with him.'

'Which gives me an idea,' Kylie murmured.

Steve regarded her quizzically. 'I do believe you are dreaming up some more ways to risk your pretty neck!'

Kylie's eyes shone. Chin lifting in that gesture he was beginning to know so well, she said, 'Maybe so. But I think I know of a way to lure Saviko out of his lair.'

Steve's mouth twitched. 'And how do you propose to do that?'

Kylie drew a deep breath. 'Suppose we were to spread the word that I had insisted the police come back and arrest Saviko? Wouldn't he try and stop me?'

'It's possible.' Steve frowned, looking at her. 'But we couldn't be sure of it.'

'But it *is* possible?' Kylie sounded so eager that Steve had to smile.

He nodded. 'It's possible. But he wouldn't necessarily have to come himself. He could send someone else.'

'But if he knew I was all alone?' queried Kylie.

'And how are you going to achieve that? Send poor Mr Carvalho packing, after all his hard work? And there's Anna Marie and that young Italian ...'

'But if he heard they had all gone, that I'd done just that? Got rid of all of them? Wouldn't he come then, Steve, thirsting for revenge? After all, if I hadn't come here, he would have got his way, terrorizing the boys, knowing that even if you *had* bought the land you were far enough away to worry overmuch about what *he* was doing.'

'Confused little Kylie!' Steve grinned, shaking his head. 'That isn't the way I see it at all.'

'But,' she objected, 'he doesn't seem to bother you nearly as much as he does me! At first, that time you were talking to him, I even imagined you *liked* him. Or,' hastily amending her words, as his grin widened, 'at least respected him. Perhaps, because I *am* so new to the country, I see through him more than you do.'

'Nonsense!'

'You men all make me so *mad*,' she said angrily. 'Anyway, whatever *you* say, Steve, it's worth a try. I'll tell Mr Carvalho he can have a few days off, drive into Umbaya with his daughter, and tell Vito I won't need him either and to go with them if he wants to. Heaven only knows when they had a few days off, anyway.'

'We'll talk about it,' Steve told her, taking her arm to lead her into the house where Anna Marie had just appeared on the verandah with a tray of drinks.

It was mid-afternoon and the sun at its hottest when Steve finally agreed to her plan. Mr Carvalho joined them after a cold lunch which Kylie and Steve refused, Steve explaining that his own lunch would be waiting when he returned. The manager listened to Kylie's plan, frowning, once or twice his eyes going to Steve, as though to test his reactions. But Steve's own expression remained carefully neutral, giving nothing away. Finally, at Anna Marie's exclamation of joy at the idea of a few days away from the mine, he said, warily, 'Well, if you think it wise, Kylie. But I can't say I much care for the idea of you being here alone.'

'Papa.' Anna Marie's voice pleaded. 'It's simply ages since we were in town! And there are so many things I

122

need.'

Spreading his hands in surrender, he smiled, obviously unable to resist the girl's pleading. 'Very well, we will go. But,' his eyes shrewed and suddenly wary, he gazed at the silent man and the brooding face of the girl, 'there is more to this than meets the eye, no?'

Steve gave a short laugh. 'No. I assure you, Mr Carvalho, Kylie will be all right. I guarantee it, in fact. And a few days off will do you all the world of good.'

TWELVE

More to assuage his own fears than Kylie's, Steve insisted a couple of his men stay at the house until Mr Carvalho and the other's returned.

'If anything happens,' he warned her grimly, 'and I mean *any*thing, young lady, you are to telephone right away. Do you hear?'

Kylie nodded, trying to repress a smile. 'I do.'

'And,' he went on, just as seriously, 'you might as well know I don't approve of this harebrained scheme of yours one little bit. If I thought for one moment you would be in any danger, I'd cancel the whole thing.'

Kylie's lips lifted at the corners. 'Does it bother you, then? That I might be in possible danger? Really, Steve! What happened to all that talk of freedom and doing exactly as you like? Of the danger of permitting someone else to share your private world?'

At the light-hearted way she was treating the whole thing his face darkened in anger. Kylie felt a small chill go through her, thinking of that anger, of the way he had treated the man in the Land Rover. He caught her wrist in such a fierce grip that she cried out. She wasn't, she told herself, really frightened, for she knew he had not lost his temper and he was not the kind of man who becomes dangerous until his temper ruled him. She let herself go limp, biting into her bottom lip. Immediately he relaxed his grip and said, in a strangely gentle voice, 'I'm sorry, my dear. But don't make jokes about something you understand so little. Saviko is a ruthless man. Don't under-rate him.'

'I don't, Steve. Believe me, I don't.'

124

He left just after that, and as the Land Rover vanished in a cloud of dust Anna Marie joined her on the verandah. She watched as the red cloud slowly mingled with the warm afternoon air, then said, 'He is worried about you, no?'

'No,' replied Kylie, turning away. 'Why should he be?'

The dark girl shrugged and soon afterwards went inside to answer her father's call.

One night went by ... two, and still Saviko didn't come. Kylie had no doubt that Steve had spread the news of her intention to have the old man arrested, although, in her own private opinion, little would be done about such a request. The second night drifted into a hot day and nothing happened. Steve hadn't come again, although his boys were much in evidence; pottering in the garden, within full view of the verandah, intently weeding the grass each time she went for a dip in the icy waters of the green-fringed pool.

One of them, boasting proudly that he had cooked at one time for Boss Jamison himself, offered to run the kitchen and prepare the simple meals that was all Kylie felt she needed in this heat. Mostly cold meats and salads, followed by fresh fruit gathered from the rather neglected orchard that grew like a jungle at the back of the house.

She wrote letters. One to Paul, cheerful and full of comic description. She left out Poppy's death and the witchdoctor, concentrating on the mine itself and the women and children living in the compound. Even if, she thought wryly, in her present loneliness, she did tend to exaggerate a little.

The shrill ringing of the telephone made her jump. She ran to answer it, hoping with sudden exhilaration that it was Steve. It was. His voice, over the humming

125

wires, murmured, 'You all right, Kylie? You didn't phone me. I was—and I hate to admit it—worried about you.'

On the point of replying with something bright and sarcastic, Kylie found herself saying instead, 'I'm so glad, Steve. You being worried about me, I mean. I was beginning to think everyone had forgotten me, including Saviko, and that I was wasting my time.'

She heard his deep chuckle. 'Do I detect self-doubts? And from a girl who insists she is capable of coping with anything, predictable *or* otherwise?'

Was he, she wondered, still laughing at her? Before she could answer, he went on, 'I take it, then, from your cheerful tone, that nothing of importance has happened? How utterly frustrating!'

Now she knew he *was* being sarcastic. Her voice, as she'd answered the telephone had been anything but cheerful. Or if it had, it had been a down-right lie. Again struggling to think up an answer, she heard him say, '*You* accepted the challenge, you know. You were the one to suggest the whole thing.'

She said, breathing hard, 'There is no need to antagonize me, Steve Jamison. I'm not complaining. I merely said . . .'

'That you were glad I was worried about you. All right, I admit to having a few, a very few, human weaknesses. I'd probably feel the same way about a lost dog . . .'

'Really!' Kylie's cheeks burned. Then the thought came to her. He was baiting her. As she'd suspected before, Steve Jamison was a woman hater. He delighted cutting them down to size, wanting to humiliate her for being so resolute on what she was trying to prove.

Her voice was icy as she said, 'Well, thank's for the call, but I really am all right. I'll phone you as soon as anything, *if* anything, happens.'

She heard his urgent, 'Kylie . . . !' as she replaced the receiver, her mouth suddenly trembling. She fumbled with the handle of her bedroom door, feeling suddenly weary. A headache threatened as a roll of thunder, still miles away, rumbled on the horizon, echoing over and over again as it rolled across the spine of the mountain range, looking absurdly like the back of some prehistoric monster against the darkening sky.

An hour later Steve's boys came to her, glancing pointedly up at the clouds, now almost as dark as midnight. They said, 'Better if we go to our houses now, Miss Kylie. It will rain too much.' They looked at her, assessing the effect of their request by her frown. Instead she smiled. 'Of course. You'll both get awfully wet if you don't go now. I can manage my own supper. There are plenty of things in the fridge. Don't worry,' as one, the self-assigned cook, began to voice a half-hearted protest. No doubt thinking back to Steve's stern admonishment of staying near her always.

The two Africans had slept on the verandah, turn about, rolled up in a blanket and within calling distance. She thought Steve had probably insisted on this. But tonight this would be asking too much. The open verandah, protected only by fine wire gauze and a low brick wall, would give little shelter from the threatened rainstorm. She really couldn't expect that of the two boys, good-natured as they were.

She watched them go, hurrying to avoid the heavy drops of rain, large as dollar pieces. Scattered at first, rapidly increasing to a downpour, drumming on the corrugated-iron roof so that it seemed as if the drums were once again in her head, all about her.

She made a pot of tea and a sandwich, closing the door leading from the verandah to the lounge, wishing there was a lock and not just an old-fashioned handle, and sat huddled in a chair, suddenly chilled, unwilling to brave the darkness of her room to fetch a cardigan. The pressure-lamp there was difficult to light at the best of times, sometimes flickering for ages before she could pump it into a good glow. The idea of standing in that small, dark room, fiddling with the damned thing didn't appeal to her, even though she *was* cold and longed to wrap the warm softness of the new shawl Poppy had insisted on making for her just before her . . .

She shied away from the thought. She was alone in the house, she thought. And suddenly very conscious of it. It wasn't only Steve who was afraid for her—if she could believe his words. She was afraid for herself. She turned on the old-fashioned radio. But the static was so bad that she turned it off again. She couldn't concentrate on a book and after a few minutes threw it across the room in a sudden rage. Chiding herself for being such a ninny, she told herself to go to bed. Surely no one, not even a man such a Saviko, would be foolish enough to brave this storm? Undressing in the dark, she lay down, first fetching another blanket from the cupboard in the bathroom. The extra warmth made her drowsey and she soon slept.

She woke to silence and a darkness lit by a pale watery moon. The rain had stopped. The sudden silence must have wakened her. She closed her eyes, willing herself to sink back to sleep. But sleep would be neither threatened or cajoled. The deep silence of the night seemed suddenly oppressive, and the wind, blowing at the window, shaking the trees, was a dark figure wrapped in a blanket, standing, waiting in the shadows . . .

She sat up in bed, wide awake, as a sound came from the lounge. Something falling . . . With a frantic movement she threw the bedclothes from her, her thoughts going back to the evening of the summer-house, the flames leaping and curling like messengers of death. Slipping swiftly into slacks and a jersey, she ran along the passage, expecting to see the whole house ablaze, the curtains flaring up at the windows, the blaze gathering everything within its reach.

She never heard Saviko, but suddenly the dark hooded figure was there before her, taller than she remembered. She stopped, for one brief moment frozen where she stood. She knew panic would be fatal. A scream rose in her throat and a desire to run and keep running. But she was beyond screaming. Beyond hope. Her knees suddenly giving way beneath her weight, she sunk onto the low settee, praying, 'Please God, don't let it be too agonizing, let it be over soon . . .'

'I have been waiting for you, Miss Graham.' Kylie gasped at the coolness of his tone. She thought, her biggest mistake, when the two boys decided to sleep in the servants' quarters at the far end of the garden was not to telephone Steve. She should have done. Of course she should have done. She'd been a fool not to . . . And the fire? A dream . . .

Saviko was talking again, the almost toothless mouth leering at her in the dim light of the moon. 'Now that we are alone perhaps we can talk at last.'

'Talk?' Kylie's lips tightened, fear pumping adrenaline into her bloodstream, giving her courage. 'I have no intention of talking to you, Saviko. The police will do that.'

'We will talk.' The old man's voice was firm. 'There is no one here with you. No one can stop me killing you if I have a mind to.'

'We're not alone, Saviko.' Kylie's own voice sounded weak and strained in her ears, the sudden spurt of courage already dissipated. 'You're crazy if you think I would be left alone in this house. You had better give

129

yourself up. The police would dearly love to question you in regard to Poppy's murder.'

Her words sounded limp and foolish even as she said them. Where, she thought, was Steve? Wasn't he supposed to be watching out for such a contingency?

Saviko laughed and took a few steps nearer. 'You refer, I suppose, to your maid. You are quite right, Miss Graham, although I did not actually do the killing, I gave the orders for it . . .'

'But why?' Kylie frowned at him. 'What had Poppy done to you?'

'She was a traitor to her own people. She would not do as I bid, and the people here know what that means, but there was no other way, believe me.'

As he talked, Kylie looked about for something to throw, something to use as a weapon. There was only the brass lamp beside her on the low table. She seized it, lifted it in her hand and—and flung it just as Saviko turned away.

'You'll hang for that, you old devil,' she screamed. 'Keep away . . .'

The lamp hit him on one shoulder, glancing off and crashing to the floor. The witchdoctor's eyes gleamed malevolently in the darkness. 'You, too, are capable of violence, I see,' he snarled. 'And regardless of what you say, you *are* alone in the house. Do not try to deny it. I saw the two men who worked for your father leave with the girl. Do not try to fool me, Miss Graham. I am far wiser in many ways than you could ever know.'

Thinking of the effect that the dream of the fire had had upon her, Kylie had to agree. Wise, he certainly was. But wise in evil, devilish things, probably passed down for generations. A type of hypnotism . . . she wondered . . .

'Even if they have gone,' she said, trying to sound

130

calm, 'they will be back soon. By early daylight . . .'

His lips twisted in scorn. 'Do not lie to me, woman. No one who knows these mountain roads would be foolish enough to drive on them during the hours of darkness. Perhaps they will be back by morning, but you will no longer be here. By then you will be miles away—or dead. Depending entirely upon yourself.'

Kylie went cold. He gazed at her in silence for a few moments, and then said, 'Get up! We must go.'

Her knees felt weak as she walked slowly to the screen door. 'Where are we going? And,' turning to face him, 'what makes you think I'll go with you, anyway?'

He produced a wicked looking knife, the blade stained a rusty red. He held it inches from her throat. 'This makes me think, woman. Now go.'

As she went down the steps from the verandah the point of the knife never left her back. Once, her feet firm on the ground, she thought of running, knowing that once she was away it would be easy to elude the old man. For all his agility he would never be a match for Kylie in that dark maze of bushes that was the garden. But as though reading her thoughts, Saviko pressed the knife point harder against her back. Carefully she picked her way across the garden, avoiding the larger rain puddles, her shoes sinking in the soft mud left by the tropical downpour.

There would be another opportunity. There had to be, or she would have to create one. She would be risking death to do so, but if she went along, without trying to escape, death would be a certainty anyway. His intention seemed to be to take her with him into the mountains. Once there, anything could happen.

Perhaps, if she cried out, one of Steve's boys in the servants' quarters would hear. But again she went cold. It could also mean their deaths.

131

Through the darkness she saw the dim shape of a car, square against the grey sky. Dawn wasn't far off and soon, she knew, the sun would be above the rim of the mountains, giving her a better chance.

The witchdoctor opened the door of the vehicle and pushed her in. Still holding the knife inches from her face he said, 'You will drive, Miss Graham.' He climbed in beside her, pointing to the keys swinging from the ignition. 'Please proceed.'

Kylie leaned forward, resting her head on her arms, spread across the steering wheel. At this outward sign of despondency, Saviko said nothing, watching in silence, content to let her take her own time. But after a few moments during which time Kylie's brain spun desperately in an endeavour to think straight, he said, and there was impatience in his voice, 'Please, Miss Graham, we must get started. It will be daylight soon.'

The knife touched her shoulder and she felt a wet stickiness begin to drip down her sleeve. 'All right,' she said, and started the engine. The car was ancient and the road they followed increasingly narrow. As the greyness of dawn began to fill the sky Kylie saw they had come to what looked like a dead end. A wall of rock that filled the road before them, cutting off any possible chance of going further.

Braking, she turned to gaze at Saviko. 'What now?' It amazed her to hear how calm and collected her own voice sounded.

'Now we walk.'

Kylie gazed at him, aghast. 'Where to?'

Gazing upwards, at the mountains all about them, he said, 'There is a camp, with men, higher up. We go to them.'

She had gone from bad to worse, she thought, taking gulps of the fresh, early morning air, improvising as she went along ... and she had done badly.

'What do you want with me?'

Saviko hissed his amusement. 'You will be held as a hostage. A valuable bargaining piece for our side ...' She heard the words end in a strangled sound. She turned her head to see the shirt-sleeved arm around Saviko's throat—the smiling eyes of Steve Jamison gazing into her's, as he crouched on the back seat of the car.

THIRTEEN

Saviko's eyes bulged. His dark face was slowly turning into a deep purple. 'Please, Steve,' Kylie heard herself say, 'he's an old man. Don't kill him.'

'I'll resist the temptation, this time,' Steve said, slowly releasing his grip, 'although I might be sorry later.'

Saviko slumped back into the seat, eyes closed, breathing harsh. He sounded so ill that Kylie became a little worried. Steve grinned. 'Don't give the old devil another thought, Kylie. He's a tough old nut. Take more than that to knock him off.'

Eyes widening, she looked at him. 'But how on earth did you know what was happening? I mean, I thought I was all alone in the house . . .'

'You were. Until that phone call.' Steve's eyes teased. 'I realized, despite your brave words to the contrary, how frightened you really were. I drove over here and made myself a bed on the verandah, the back one, so that when Saviko arrived he didn't see me. I didn't want to frighten him off. So I let events take their course and hid in the back seat of his car when I heard you talking. Which brings us up to the present.'

Kylie stared at him, cheeks flaming. 'You *heard* everything he said and you let me go through with it? I was a sort of—bait?'

Steve nodded, eyes fixed on the stirring witchdoctor. 'Not a very nice word, but it fits.'

'And you let me come all this way, all alone, knowing . . . ?'

'You weren't all alone. I was behind you, in the back seat.'

'Don't split hairs!' Kylie's eyes blazed. 'I was as good as alone . . .'

'To reveal my presence would have only made it worse. This way, I had the element of surprise. Sorry about it, old girl, but it was all for the best.'

Reluctantly she had to admit she supposed so. 'Even so,' she began, then heard a hiss, like a snake striking, a voice said, 'This is for you, Steve Jamison, my one-time friend,' and turning she saw Saviko sitting upright in his seat. His hand came up with the knife—lunging at Steve.

It flashed through the air. Kylie gave a sharp scream —then darkness came down on her. For the second time in her life she had fainted. She couldn't have been unconscious for more than a second or two, because when she opened her eyes she saw the figure of Saviko vanishing among the large boulders that dotted the mountainside. She sat up quickly as realization dawned. 'Steve, he's getting away . . .'

'So he is.' Steve didn't seem in the least concerned and she struggled to sit upright, feeling his hand push her firmly back in her seat. 'But, Steve . . .'

'We'll get him. Don't worry.' He peered at her in the grey morning light. 'But what about you? Are you all right?'

Her blonde head nodded, frantically. 'But the knife! He was going to . . .'

Steve took her in his arms, holding her tightly to his body. One large hand smoothed back the tangled hair from her forehead and his eyes were very tender. Not that Kylie noticed, she was too busy squinting over Steve's shoulder at the old man's progress up the hillside. Progress amazingly good for one so ancient.

Steve said, 'The old man's not much of a fighter, thank goodness. He relies more on brain than brawn.'

He grinned down into her face. Then putting her gently from him climbed out of the car. She noticed for the first time the rifle he carried, neligently, in the crook of his arm. How quickly one becomes toughened, she thought. Here it was only a few months since she had been the big city girl, hopping on and off buses and tube trains, the only excitement the monthly visit to her mother and stepfather on the back of Paul's motor bike. Since then she had seen death and evilness, barely escaping violent death herself. She felt a little proud that she had managed to meet all those things with fortitude, not going into hysterics or breaking down, near to it as she had been, at times. In fact, she felt she had become something of a veteran.

She saw Steve looking at her as she followed him onto the wet muddy roadway. 'Feel up to following the old devil?' he asked, 'if not, you can stay in the car. I want to see where he went and this camp he talked about.'

Kylie shivered and looked about her. 'I'm not staying here without you. I'll come . . .'

'It's a stiff climb,' he warned her, squinting upwards.

'I don't care. You're not leaving me here alone, Steve Jamison.'

She thought, climbing the hill at Steve's side, 'For all my bravery, I'm not anxious for any more adventure.' She merely wanted the threat of violence and the grip of the old witchdoctor removed from the vicinity of the Sheila Mine. She wanted Saviko paid back for the terror he had inflicted on her mine boys and their families. And, above all else, she wanted retribution for Poppy's death . . .

Suddenly, above them, she saw the men, Saviko and some others. The men, two Africans, were dressed in a curious uniform of dirty khaki and Steve gave a soft exclamation at sight of them. He said, bending towards her ear, 'I think Saviko's gone beyond frightening the people to gain his own ends and dishing out muti. (medicine.) Those men are terrorists.'

Kylie's face paled. The newspapers were full of stories of these so-called 'Freedom Fighters', hiding in the

136

mountains. She had never imagined they would approach so close. 'What shall we do?' She looked at him hopefully, confident that he would have the solution at his fingertips. As though reading her mind he grinned and said, 'I'm not that good! One of us will have to go back and telephone the police. They will have to know about this.'

Kylie whispered, 'Let me, Steve. I can get back . . .'

He looked amused. 'A moment ago you were pleading not to be left alone.'

'I can try.'

'It must be two miles or more, Kylie. You'd never make it. You'd be lost within minutes.' He paused, peering upwards. 'Suppose we both see just what's happening up there, and then we can both go and inform the police?'

Kylie nodded. 'Whatever you say, Steve.'

They climbed again, the slope becoming increasingly difficult, last night's rain making it almost impossible to find firm footholds. After a few minutes Steve halted her with one hand on her arm. 'It no use, Kylie. We're just tiring ourselves out. Stay here a moment and catch your breath. I'm going to see if there's an easier way up.'

She opened her mouth to protest but he pushed her into a deep crevasse. 'If you hear any noises stay put and get as far into this cleft as you can.'

Looking at her pale face he thought of the terrorists, of the weapons they undoubtably carried and almost changed his mind. Kylie would be left at their mercy if anything happened to him. His sudden concern for her made him angry and he turned abruptly away, going caterwise across the steep hill slope.

Kylie watched him going, watched as he vanished behind some huge boulders higher up the slope. Then she saw Saviko. He was standing above her, out of Steve's view. He gazed upwards to where Steve climbed, shading

137

his eyes with one hand from the brightness of the coming day. He turned and beckoned to someone behind him, and Kylie saw the two men, both carrying automatic weapons, appear from the rocks. They conversed in low tones, Saviko pointing upwards to where Steve's figure was just visible among the rocks. Kylie held her breath.

It would be so easy; a quick burst of gunfire and Steve would be no more. 'Please God, no,' she prayed, and leaving the protection of the crevasse began to climb towards them, the newly healed cuts on her hands beginning to hurt as she struggled desperately at the rocks, pulling herself up towards Steve. She dare not call out to warn him. Saviko would hear and as his prisoner once more she would be little help to either Steve or herself.

She bit her lip savagely, praying that Steve would pause long enough to look back and see them. Small stones slipped beneath her feet as she struggled for footholds. Her hands left scarlet traces of blood on the grey rocks but Kylie didn't feel the pain. Her whole being was focused on the tall figure of Steve.

Saviko advanced a few steps, their weapons pointing at Steve. Kylie screamed and her scream echoed around the hillside, distracting Saviko's attention for the moment. All that was necessary for Steve to vanish over the crest of the hill. A silence followed that was more terrifying than anything Kylie had ever known before. A silence broken by the slither of loose stones and startled, she looked up to see Vito appear from the shelter of the grove of msasas below.

Vito! Thank God! she thought, and the thought never entered her head that Vito, with Mr Carvalho and Anna Marie, was supposed to be in town, a hundred miles away. She saw he held a rifle on one arm. Her breath was coming in sobs as she fled down the rocky slope to meet him.

'My dear Miss Kylie,' he said, pausing before her, a

half smile on his good-looking face. 'We've been waiting for you.'

Turning she saw approaching behind her the two terrorists and Saviko, hurrying to join them.

He waited until they had almost reached him, then said, 'Did you imagine they would let you go? There is too much at stake and, I'm afraid, the word mercy has very little meaning in their society.' His eyes, as they looked into her own, wide startled one's, were apologetic. 'You would stay, you see. Nothing anyone said had the slightest influence on you. Even our carefully calculated accidents didn't frighten you or the mumbo-jumbo of Saviko's ghost drums.' He looked down at her, carefully cradling the rifle in one arm. 'As for Mr Jamison, well, he is also a menace about which we intend to do something. And right this minute.'

Holding her by the arm he turned to where the witch-doctor and the others stood behind him, as though waiting for orders. Their whole attention was focused on the young Italian as Kylie gave him a mighty push and as he stumbled, relinquishing her arm, she ran. Slipping and sliding on the rocky slopes she made for a thick bush nearby, thrusting her way into its thickness. But the pain was nothing to the anxiety she felt for Steve. Any moment now she would hear the shots ring out, echoing around the mountains, frightening the birds from the trees. And Steve would be no more . . .

Then something, the very ground, was sliding beneath her. A split second later there was nothing under her but the thick tops of trees growing in a deep gorge below. She grasped at a thin branch, her movements desperate, for if she was lost Steve was also lost. The branch made a bow under her weight and she fell. For a moment she hung by her hands. But the blood on them was wet and she could not hold. She crashed down, striking first the rough grey face of the rocks, then slithering an interminable way into the gorge.

For an age she lay there with her eyes closed. She was jolted and shocked and prayed for nothing more than to lie here in the sun, the aches in her body the uppermost in her mind. After a while she sat up and looked around. There was no sign of Steve or the others. She thought of them hunting him, with guns, as they would an animal.

She stood up and tested her limbs, glad to find there was nothing broken, although her ankle caused her pain when she stood on it.

'Miss Kylie!' The voice was sibilantly soft. 'You never give up, do you?' Her breath came in one long hopeless sigh as Vito appeared from the bushes above her, followed by the two men. He regarded her with pity and Kylie, unable to help herself, lunged forward, raking at him with her nails.

'No,' she flung at him, 'I never do. And if you hurt Steve I'll ...'

He held her off easily, laughing into her face. 'Who would have guessed that old man Graham's daughter could have turned out so stubborn! You see, Miss Kylie, the mine has become invaluable to us in that it acts as camouflage to our other, more important, activities.'

Fierce resentment against this man whom she had taken for a friend and who now stood before her, calmly telling her of his plans for her father's, *her* mine, rose up inside her and the urge to claw and scratch that smiling face was almost irresistible. But she must remain calm, hide her feelings as best she could and watch for a chance for escape, to find Steve and warn him of Vito's treachery.

She saw that as though weary of the talking Saviko and the two men had retired down the hill a little way, to the shade of the msasas and seemed no longer interested in the conversation. They were so very sure of

140

themselves, thought Kylie. Sure in the knowledge that they were safe, that no one knew of their presence in this isolated hill area. She longed to join them, to collapse under the msasas in the deep welcome shade, for already the sun burned down from a vividly blue sky. But she knew she must remain here, keeping Vito talking as long as she could, for while he talked to her Steve was safe.

But as though reading her mind he took her arm once more and calling to the men below began to pull Kylie along with him. Although her ankle threatened to give in she marched resolutely along with him, determined not to show that she was afraid. It seemed ages later when, almost dropping from exhaustion, she heard Vito call for the men who marched ahead to stop. Ahead she saw a small cave-mouth opening before them. Inside it smelt of damp earth and animals and Vito thrust her forward, saying abruptly, 'Sit down. Rest. I'll find you some water to drink.'

'Don't bother,' she told him, scathingly, and he shrugged, turning from her to uncap a water bottle and held it to his own mouth. The other men drank greedily, the water flowing down their chins onto their shirts and later Saviko approached her. 'You were not so clever as you thought, Miss Graham,' he said, 'we still have our hostage, and Mr Jamison in the bargain.'

'You still have to find him,' she taunted him, eyes flashing. 'What makes *you* think you're *that* clever?'

He shrugged and wandered away, to join the others in the cave entrance.

After a few minutes Kylie stretched out on the blanket Vito had given her, with instructions to get some rest. She heard the voices by the entrance and once or twice Steve's name, and shivered. Where *was* Steve? she wondered. Finding her gone, had he gone back to the house to phone the police? She realized she was dreadfully tired but knew she must keep awake. There must be a

141

way to get out of this mess!

Eyes wide open, she lay and listened to the men's voices as they talked. Not to succumb to exhaustion and sleep, that was the important thing. But her eyes became too heavy to remain open and she forced herself to sit up, clasping her drawn-up knees with her arms. Her ankle was still swollen and tender and she rubbed it absently, her thoughts with Steve, wherever he was.

For some time she had noticed, as her eyes became accustomed to the darkness of the cave, an area of lighter darkness further down the cave. It seemed to come from a fissure high up in the roof, a sort of shaft and as she rose and went quietly over to it, she could feel fresh air blowing down on her face. She turned to peer at the men in the cave entrance but they were too engrossed in what sounded to her almighty like a fierce argument to notice her.

She could hear Saviko's voice, high-pitched, like the angry buzzing of a bee above the others. Vito's sounded calmer, as though trying to reason with them. As she moved further away from the entrance she saw that the walls on either side were packed high with boxes. Fresh, new wooden crates with black markings on the sides . . .

So she didn't dream it? There had been crates in the summer-house after all! Slowly she went forward. Equipment of every description lay on the sandy floor. Bending, she picked up a heavy crowbar, testing its weight in her hand, gingerly. Not bad! she thought. If the chance to use it came, well, she would be only too delighted to oblige. Her mouth tightened. Especially on Vito Versini, she thought, bitterly.

The voices behind her became loud and she turned, hurrying back to her blanket to hide the crowbar beneath one of its corners. In spite of her efforts to stay awake she must however have fallen asleep for when next she woke there was no sign of the two terrorists and

Saviko, only Vito sitting in the cave entrance, knees drawn up, one hand holding the rifle.

As she moved he got up and stood the rifle against the wall, coming over to her. 'I'm glad you were able to sleep, Miss Kylie. You look so pale, so fatigued. Won't you have a drink now?'

'All right.' The cave was so hot, so smelly that although she hated to accept any favour from this man she felt if she didn't have a drink of water soon she would die. Afterwards she said, looking straight at him, 'What do you plan to do with me? You must know I'll do my damnest to get away and report you. And the only way you're going to stop me doing that is by killing me.'

He looked pained. 'I must confess the thought had crossed our minds but, on the other hand, these mountains are so extensive that if we turned you loose without food or water, within twenty-four hours you would be dead anyway. If not from exhaustion then from wild animals. Leopards abound here. You could not escape, you know. And although the idea of killing you is torture to me, there are so many ways it would make your head spin just by listening to them.'

Under the corner of the blanket Kylie's fingers closed on the heavy crowbar. She smiled. 'Tell me about them?' she murmured, watching his face, judging the distance from the rifle to where he stood beside her, looking down. His smile was mocking in the dim light.

'So many ways,' he said, 'but Saviko has decided otherwise. Unless, of course, you are foolish enough to antagonize him, and then he would have no pity. You will be held as hostage. Recently the police sentenced four of our top men to long terms of jail. You, my dear Miss Kylie, will be exchanged for their freedom. Your life for theirs . . .'

The smile remained there, for an instant, when she hit him with the crowbar, springing to her feet with a swiftness that took him by surprise. She sprung round him, making for the cave entrance, praying that the other three men had wandered away for the moment, for there had been no sign or sound of them.

Then she was fleeing across the open space outside the cave before Vito recovered sufficiently to come after her. Looking back, she saw him, stumbling clumsily, nevertheless he carried the rifle. She hadn't hit him hard enough, she told herself regretfully. The blow must have been a glancing one for the crowbar was heavy enough to put him out completely otherwise.

She sped down the hillside, seeing in the distance the scarlet msasas, praying that she would reach their sheltering foliage before Vito caught up with her. Out here on the sunlit mountainside it was so open. There at least the thick trunks would offer some protection, if only a little. he heard his voice—'Miss Kylie, don't be foolish . . . Listen to me . . .'

Her breath came painfully, so painfully it hurt. Black spots danced before her eyes. The trees were so near now, only a few yards away. Vito was dragging a little and she thought, hopefully, perhaps she *had* hit him harder than she had imagined. Then suddenly she could go no further. The thick trunk of a tree was before her and she clung to it, sobbing for breath.

'Miss Kylie,' Vito called again. 'Be reasonable. We weren't going to harm you, not really. I had instructions merely to frighten you . . .'

Suddenly Vito halted. His eyes narrowed. 'All right! I lied. You are to be allowed to go. If you follow the track through the trees you will come to the roadway. The car you came in cannot be far away . . .'

The hand holding the rifle shifted, one finger feeling for the trigger. He would wait until she was clear of the trees, in the bright sunlight that would silhouette her figure perfectly . . .

Tomorrow when, and if, the police came, he would explain that she and Mr Jamison had insisted on following Saviko into the mountains. He had arrived back at the house a day or two before Mr Carvalho and found them gone. A search would be sent out but no trace of them would ever be found. It would become yet another mystery, filed away in some cabinet, to be discussed over sun-downers for a month or two, then forgotten. Two people, lost in the mountains, perfect foil for wild animals . . .

But why didn't she run? he wondered. She stood there, grasping the tree trunk, her breathing fast returning to normal, but yet she made no move to run. The trees grew too thickly together to enable him to take a shot at her now. At the sound of a shot Saviko and his men would come running and they might not be as casual about her death as he. No, if she would just run out from the shelter of the trees. Just enough to allow him to . . .

For what seemed an eternity Kylie hesitated, trying to read his mind, wondering what new trick he was up to. The sun scorched the back of her neck and the bare patch of skin on one shoulder displayed by the torn shirt. The slight wound, made by Saviko's knife, had stopped bleeding long ago, but it was painful now, smarting as the sun burned down on her. Irrationally, she felt dismay at the state of the shirt, torn beyond repair by the old man's knife. Her ankle throbbed and she knew she would not be able to go far, not with that ankle.

She hadn't the faintest hope of escape and yet, strangely enough, she was not afraid. Once more she heard Vito's call, telling her she was free, why did she not go? The words seemed to wake some inner self and with half a sob, she released her hold on the tree and began running. Her progress was slow now, a mere stumble between the trees. Vito watched her, a frown on his handsome face, then, as though against his will,

145

lifted the rifle to one shoulder, taking aim.

Unaware of his act, Kylie ran, feeling the injured ankle giving beneath her weight, almost throwing her to the ground. She had reached an open patch of ground where the going was easier. She was not to know that this was what Vito had been waiting for.

A loose stone rolled beneath her foot and she stumbled, falling to the ground. She lay there sobbing and it was at this instant that Vito fired. The rifle shot reverberated through the mountains, the echo following, seeming twice as loud. The three men down the mountainside paused and Saviko muttered angrily. Without a word they started back up the rocky incline, coming upon Vito as he was about to take fresh aim.

The witchdoctor uttered an explosive oath and broke into a stumbling run, followed by the two men. Kylie heard him call in a breathless voice for Vito to stop. Almost hysterically, the young Italian turned towards them, the rifle still held at his shoulder. 'She must be stopped,' he screamed. 'She must be stopped, if we are to go ahead with our plans without interference from the police.'

Saviko shouted and almost petulently Vito lowered the rifle, holding it loosely in one arm, glaring mutinously at the witchdoctor. 'I don't understand you, old man,' he muttered. 'I understood if she escaped she was to be killed. Together with this Steve Jamison. Now you tell me no. If you do not know your own mind, how then, can any of us know it?'

Silently Kylie inched her way across the dusty, rock-hard ground. She hadn't the faintest idea where she could hide, but at least she was putting *some* distance between herself and the men, even if it was only negligable. She sensed the acrimony between the men. There was every sign that any moment now it would flair into open rebellion, on Vito's part, at least, and then would be her chance to vanish.

Vanish where? she thought. She could feel the dust on her face, mingling with the perspiration that ran down from her hairline, into her eyes, tasting salty on her lips. She wondered if she would ever feel clean or cool again. Indeed, she'd almost forgotten what it was like to feel cold, and it was an effort to drag her mind back from the thought of mist and the cool soft rain of an English summer.

The three men were arguing again. She could hear their raised voices as she reached the edge of the trees and saw before her an open space. She paused but didn't turn round. If Vito was taking aim again it was better if she didn't know.

The open patch of ground was deceptively small, leading into a narrow ravine into which Kylie crawled, lowering herself as far as she could into the litter of dry leaves that almost filled it. The men's voices faded and finally become a blur and she wondered why they had allowed her to escape so easily.

The narrow ravine led into a wider one and here she could stand, holding onto the rocky sides as she went. There were massive boulders, some balancing so precariously on others that she shuddered, remembering the 'sacred' place and Poppy's body . . . Creepers and spindly trees grew out of crevices. There was no sound but the occasional snap of a stick and now and again the flight of some small creature frightened by her progress.

She thought with some trepidation of the leopards Vito had mentioned and kept a sharp look-out. The sun was dropping fast and she knew she had little time before darkness. Once she thought she heard the faint sound of a shout and paused to listen, her heart hammering so loudly she could hear no other sound but that, anyway. She grimaced and forced herself to lean against the side of a huge boulder. Warmed by the sun until it was almost scorching to the touch, she quickly stood upright and pushed her way forward. Her ankle hurt so much now she hobbled, but tried not to think of it, only of escape—and Steve.

Surely he must be back at the house by now, having telephoned the police? Either that or . . . But she refused to let her mind dwell on the possibility.

Then the muffled cry came again and she turned eagerly, sure she would see Steve behind her, her thoughts having conjured him up. It was only the thought of Steve that had kept her going, she realized. Staring back along the ravine through which she had come, her heart sank. It wasn't Steve but Vito. His hair was untidy, hanging over his eyes, his face flushed and somehow wild looking. Even as she halted, her courage melting under the hatred in those eyes, he raised the rifle he carried to his shoulder.

She could run no more. Quietly she waited, slumped against a rock, the sunlit scene blurring before her eyes so that she didn't see the hands that reached out from the rocks beside her and grasped at her arms.

She screamed as the rifle in Vito's hands went off and at the same time the hands dragged her downward.

FOURTEEN

'Kylie!' whispered Steve and one arm tightened around her. 'Don't panic, it's me. I saw you coming along the path through the ravine. I've been waiting for you to catch up but didn't want Vito to see me.'

Kylie ceased struggling. She looked into his eyes and the whole world steadied, became sane again. Vito's second shot careened off the top of the boulder behind which they crouched, and flattened itself against another.

Steve pressed her down, into the leaf carpeted ground. 'Keep your head down,' he muttered, softly, utterly calm, as though they were out for a country walk instead of fighting for their very lives.

'Steve!' she began, desperation in her voice, but he grinned down at her, shaking his head. 'Later, honey. Lots of time for explanation later.'

Vito fired a third time, taking deliberate aim, carefully taking his time and this was the moment Steve was waiting for. He stood and Kylie saw for the first time the rifle and cringed as he pulled the trigger, holding it steadily to his shoulder. An enormous explosion roared in her ears and when next she looked Vito was falling, the rifle clattering on the rocky ground below him. Vito followed it, rolling, floundering down the slope until he came crossways against a large rock.

Kylie felt Steve move away from her. She screamed, 'No, Steve! The others could be watching ...' They, too, were armed. 'Oh, don't go, darling. Please come back ...'

Turning a white face towards her, Steve said, 'Stay where you are, Kylie. I've got to know for sure about him. *Stay where you are.*' For, regardless of his warning

Kylie was scrabbling across the dusty ground to where he crouched. She watched as he walked slowly to where Vito lay, her eyes raking the mountain above her for signs of the other men.

But there were none and when a few moments later Steve joined her she was crying, great sobs shaking her slim body, the tears making a white trail down her dusty cheeks. In the silence his hands touched her face, brushing away the tears and his voice, very gently, said, 'He's dead, Kylie. It was quick. I doubt if he felt anything.'

The full force of the day's terror took its toll of her at his words, the gentleness of his touch sparking it off like a match. She collapsed in his arms, the sobs growing louder as he patted her back, saying, 'There, there, darling. It's all over . . . all over . . .'

He got her away from the rocks and they scrambled slowly along the wide ravine, Kylie's sobs gradually dying away. She said, 'Somehow I felt so sorry for him, Steve. I shouldn't have, should I? He wanted to kill us . . .'

From far away in the distance came the howl of a dog, showing that they could not be too far from an African village or a homestead of sorts.

'Come on,' Steve grinned, trying to take her mind off the terrible happenings on the mountainside, 'we'll soon be home.'

The sky slowly turned to indigo, the shadows long black fingers across the rocky slopes all about them. She gave one last look behind her as they reached the bottom of the slope and so onto flat ground. They rested for a while, leaning against the still sun-warmed rocks, and Kylie told him of what had happened.

'Vito thought he was onto a good thing,' Steve commented when she finished talking. 'He didn't know the way the African mind works. That's where he come unstuck. Even if he'd lived they wouldn't have trusted

150

him. Not Saviko and the bunch he's running with. They plan for the whole country, not some of it.' His smile was bitter. 'Vito was way out of his league.'

In the darkness Kylie moved her head to look at him. 'I must confess I'm still in the dark as to what happened, Steve, and why. What was Vito hoping to gain, anyway?'

Steve began to tell her something of what he'd suspected for months.

'They wanted your mine, Kylie, wanted you off it. That way they were free to continue with their plans without interference. They were not to know that had you disposed of it I would have bought it, anyway ...'

'And poor Vito got caught in the middle of it,' said Kylie, sadly, 'and paid highly for it.'

Steve was tense. 'I didn't enjoy doing it, you know?'

'Oh, Steve, of course you didn't. I didn't mean that.'

But he was getting to his feet, pulling her up after him. 'Come on, these mountains are not the healthiest place to be after dark, and already we've wasted enough time.'

She could feel his tenseness as they walked, and thought what a puzzling man he was. But after a while it became the tenseness of being alert, of watching and listening for sounds—and not the other tenseness he'd shown when she was talking of Vito. Presently even their slow progress became too much for Kylie and she collapsed on a rock, looking up at him white-faced.

'I can't go another step, Steve, I just *can't* ... My ankle ...'

He frowned and bent to her ankle, his fingers gentle as they touched the puffy flesh about her ankle. 'Why on earth didn't you say?'

Quick tears appeared in her eyes. Her voice rose in irritable fashion.

'I didn't want to slow us down.'

151

He could see she had had enough. He got to his feet and looked about him, searching for a place suitable to spend the rest of the night. The village they had been hoping for hadn't materialized, neither had they come upon the road at the foot of the mountains and thus the hopes of a car or truck. He knew they were completely, hopelessly lost. Not only that, there was always the risk they would stumble on the two terrorists and Saviko in their wanderings. He knew Kylie had gone beyond rational thinking and could take very little more. Finally he tore down foliage of the msasa trees and made a sort of mattress in the overhang of a large boulder. It was as good a place as any. There was no food or water but that was something they could do nothing about.

Steve asked, looking down into her tear-stained eyes, 'Feeling better?'

Snuggling down into the fresh leaves Kylie gave him a tired smile.

'Much better.'

After that she slept as if she had been drugged. Towards dawn she wakened. Steve wasn't there. Sitting up, she threw off his safari jacket that sometime in the night he had placed over her body, and stood up. Steve could be far away, she told herself. He just *couldn't* be . . .

She thought she would probably have erupted into hysterics if a few moments later he hadn't appeared, carrying handfuls of green figs. He gave her some, grinning. 'I noticed the tree as I woke this morning. Still a bit green. Don't eat too many or you could end up with a sore tummy.'

'Delicious!' Kylie felt the juices of the wild figs tingle in her mouth, easing the extreme dryness that since awakening had become torture. 'I've never tasted anything quite so delicious in all my life.'

He looked pleased. 'And,' he went on, looking like a

152

conjurer producing a rabbit from a hat, 'I've discovered something else that will delight you. A stream. Not much of a one, I'll admit. But I tasted the water and it's fresh, so at least we can finish our breakfast in style and have a wash into the bargain.'

'Heavenly!' Suddenly the world wasn't such a bad place after all, she thought. The warm sunlit morning, fresh fruit, cool water and a man she . . .

At that point she stopped, seeing Steve's eyes smiling down at her, his hands held out to pull her to her feet. And it seemed as natural as breathing for him to pull her to him, putting his arms round her and kissing her. But this kiss was different, not at all like the time he kissed her in his home, in that beautiful place overlooking the valley. This was warm and tender and infinitely vitalizing, giving her strength to face whatever lay ahead.

The water in the little stream was icy cold, coming as it did from far up the mountain. Steve bathed her ankle, soaking his handkerchief in the freezing water and tying it around it. They drank some and ate some more figs. By the middle of the morning they had reached a native village and the ancient chief lent them his car, a battered heap of rusty iron dating from the war. But to Kylie, sinking her weary body on its unsprung tattered seat, Steve beside her, two of the chief's men in the back, whose instructions were to return the car, it seemed like the height of luxury.

She was surprised to see the mine truck parked outside the house and Mr Carvalho waiting for her. 'The police got in touch with us,' he explained. 'We've had parties out all night, searching for you.'

Later, bathed and changed into clean clothes, Kylie joined the men on the verandah. Anna Marie sat with them. Steve looked unbelievably fresh and rested. It was amazing, she thought, what an ice-cold beer could do for

153

a man! Kylie drunk the hot coffee Anna Marie had made for her, promising to eat a more substantial breakfast later while the dark girl applied a cold compress to her injured ankle and skilfully bandaged it. Kylie looked down at the glossy dark head in amazement. It was totally out of character and she wondered just what had prompted the gesture. Then she remembered the other times the girl had been kind to her and wondered if anyone had told her yet about Vito.

'Thank you, Anna Marie. It feels wonderful. It's very kind of you.'

The girl sprung to her feet, lips pressed tightly together, as though already regretting her benevolent gesture. Steve grinned and caught Kylie's eye, halting the swift response that sprung to her lips. Ignoring Anna Marie's sulky expression and prompted by Mr Carvalho, she began to talk of her experience on the mountain. She still had not heard the full story of Steve's absense, when she had been in the cave with the three men. Her voice grew soft as she spoke of Vito and she saw the manager's quick glance at Steve when she reached the point of his death. Anna Marie had wandered away and Kylie wondered if she knew.

'It couldn't be avoided,' Mr Carvalho murmured. 'It would have been either him or you. I understand perfectly.' He sighed. 'I always knew there was something behind that cool, smoothly efficient exterior. He was in the perfect position to organize, with Saviko, ways of scaring you off, Kylie. Possibly to frighten the mine boys into striking, thus lowering the mine's output. Finally he would have sent you home, disillusioned and frightened and wanting to be free of the Sheila Mine.'

'And there then were the cases of arms and ammunition I found in the cave,' Kylie said, remembering. 'They had probably been using the summer-house up until then, maybe before carrying it up to the cave.' A thought struck her. 'But wouldn't someone have discovered it before now? Anna Marie used the pool a lot and the summer-house was right near.'

Seeing the dull red flush appear on the mine manager's face, the dreadful suspicion in his eyes, Steve said, before anyone could say anything, 'We guessed about the arms cache. For a long time we'd known there was something hidden in those mountains, and that Saviko was probably behind it. What we didn't know was where.' At Kylie's startled look he grinned. 'Oh, yes, I've been working in collaboration with the police for some time on this little lot. The difficulty was catching them. What made it really difficult, almost impossible, was that most of the local people, the mine workers and their families, were terrified of Saviko and wouldn't split for fear of their lives. We had to find some way of flushing him out. With him caught, it would be a simple matter getting the rest of the gang. So,' smiling at the puzzlement on Kylie's face, 'there had to be some kind of bait. Something that would tempt him into the open.'

Kylie said, 'And I fell into the trap by suggesting I stay at the house alone?' Admire as she must Steve's ways of doing things, she didn't think it quite the laughing matter that he seemed to think. The very unpleasant hours that she had put in with some very unpleasant people certainly was no laughing matter. A feeling of injustice stirred within her. Steve had deliberately *lost* her, calmly and nonchalantly, to draw the enemy, knowing they would not kill her but use her as a hostage. To bargain for the lives of their own kind already in prison . . .

Unfortunately they had not bargained for Vito's wild behaviour and the fact that he had very nearly killed her. 'And that's what you left me to be, Steve Jamison,' she said aloud, her voice accusing.

'To be what?' He watched her over the rim of his

155

glass, the teasing smile in his eyes almost making her choke. He didn't give a damn, she thought. That kiss had meant nothing. His heart hadn't been involved at all, his seeming affection the spontaneous reaction of an attractive man unable to resist an easy conquest. All he wanted was to get the whole unpleasant episode over as quickly as possible and return to his quiet, well-ordered life unencumbered by silly little girl's straight out from England . . .

Her cheeks reddened. 'You left me as a hostage—or whatever you like to call it. Or should the word be decoy? You didn't give a damn whether I was frightened or—or hurt or anything . . .'

Her voice trailed away, choking in her throat and from Mr Carvalho came sounds of dismay—a soft tch, tch of his tongue. Steve leaned forward, placing the empty glass on the table. He gazed at her in surprise.

'You were never in any danger,' he told her bluntly. 'You were in safe hands.'

'Was I now?' The sarcasm in Kylie's voice was very apparent. 'Whose hands?'

Steve sighed. 'I was never far away, Kylie. Believe me! I watched every move, once they had found you. While you were in the cave I went back to the house to phone the police, but apart from that I was near you the whole time.'

Kylie stared. 'If you'd only given me some sign, something to know you were near, I wouldn't have been nearly so scared.'

'How could I? I wasn't to know how you would react. A hysterical woman on my hands was the last thing I needed right then. You might have given the whole game away. I knew Vito was with you and thought you would be safe with him. I went to find a spot higher up, above the cave, and it must have been then you hit him and ran off. I apologize for that, Kylie. I really did

156

think you were safe with Vito.'

'He left us yesterday,' Mr Carvalho explained. 'He said he had forgotten something important and would find his own way back to the mine. I wondered at the time . . .' His voice died away, then he added, softly, 'I know Anna Marie was upset about it. She had planned to . . .'

What Anna Marie had planned Kylie would never know, for at that moment a police truck appeared in the driveway, followed by a Land Rover riding in a cloud of dust. In the Land Rover Kylie could see three white police officials. She watched, getting to her feet, as the first vehicle, the truck, stopped below the verandah. Half a dozen African police got out and called something up to the small group on the verandah.

Mr Carvalho said, looking at Steve, 'They've got Vito's body . . .'

Anna Marie appeared from one corner of the house. Whether their voices had carried or just that Anna Marie had been curious, Kylie was never to know, but she watched as the lovely dark girl came towards them, walking in her usual swinging hip fashion—until her eyes caught sight of the blanket-wrapped body inside the truck. She stopped as though struck by some sudden, forceful blow, putting one hand to her mouth. Then with a wild cry, and before anyone could stop her, she ran to the open truck, bending over the body of Vito, turning one corner of the blanket back . . .

Her scream rent the air. She was no longer beautiful. The expression of fear and frustrated fury was ugly to see. 'I'll kill them,' she screamed. She began to hammer on the floor of the truck with her clenched fists. 'I'll kill them.'

Mr Carvalho went over to her, bending to say, quietly, 'Anna Marie, Quirida! Please come away. Don't torment yourself.'

The girl shook her head, her eyes glazed, gazing at her father with something akin to hatred in their lovely depths. Kylie knew she blamed him for Vito's death. Why, she didn't know. Only that the dark girl rested the blame fairly and squarely on her father's shoulders and that one day he would have to pay the price.

She shivered, and felt Steve's arms go round her, holding her close to his side. The gesture was strangely comforting. Together they stared at the little scene below them, at the stark white face of Anna Marie. She no longer possessed a capacity for reasoning. Her father still bending over her, she gave a short, high-pitched cry and flew at him. Despair had given her an amazing strength and she was beating at the big man with her fists. He grabbed her by the wrists but she twisted free. Steve left Kylie's side and closed in on them and a sense of urgency, a sort of fanaticism, seemed to sweep over her and before anyone could stop her she darted past them and ran across the garden, making for the path leading up the hillside.

Steve made as if to go after her but Mr Carvalho stopped him. 'Do not worry,' he said, and his calmness amazed Kylie. 'She will not go far. I'll see if I can catch her, reason with her . . .'

Kylie went down the wooden steps to the garden, joining Steve. Together they looked after the man as he followed the progress of his daughter through the garden, disappearing into the growth of the msasas that carpeted the hill.

Steve said, slowly, 'She's demented, unbalanced.' He gazed down at Kylie, white-faced and trembling, the whole horrible chain of events beginning at last to take their toll. His arm went round her and they went back to the verandah, where the police officials waited, on their faces looks of sympathy.

After the usual questions, Steve told them, 'If you

158

want to hear anything else, I suggest we drive into Umbaya later on in the week and Miss Graham will be in a better position to help you. As you can see, she's pretty shook up and I really don't think she's in any condition to answer any more questions now.'

After they had gone, Mr Carvalho and his daughter travelling with them, for he had brought her back, weeping and disheveled, agreeing with them that a doctor should examine her, Steve said, 'She may even need psychiatric treatment . . .'

Suddenly desperately sorry for the girl, Kylie whispered, 'What will happen to her, Steve, if she does?'

'A home of some sort. They'll take good care of her, Kylie.' He drew her closer and together they stood, gazing out onto the sun-swept garden.

'I'm sorry about the whole business. I mean, the way I treated you,' Steve said ruefully. 'I dare say you'll be going back home now.'

'Good God, no!' Kylie laughed. 'You wouldn't expect me to, would you? Give up now, after all that?'

Steve raised his eyebrows and smiled. 'You've learned a thing or two, I think, although you're still as stubborn as ever.'

She turned and looked at him. Their eyes locked. 'And, no doubt, the fiancé will be joining you any day?' Steve said, 'so you won't be entirely on your own.'   .

Kylie shook her head. 'No, Steve, he won't. He's not coming.'

Steve frowned. He started to speak but Kylie stopped him with an up-raised hand. 'Listen, Steve,' she said. 'I've lived here long enough now to know I won't ever want to go back. Even if things *are* tough, I'll stick it out. But, of course, that means you won't ever get the Sheila Mine, add it to your property . . .'

Steve looked at her and then out at the garden. 'There are other ways of getting a thing than paying money for it,' he said.

Her eyes twinkled. 'You mean, go into partnership?'

'Something like that.'

They gazed out across the garden, to where the msasas glowed in the sunlight. Oh, Poppy, thought Kylie. All this is a requiem for you. The waters close over so quickly, with no ripple to show that you've ever been. She looked up at the mountain, at the grey rocks and thorn bushes as well as the lovely scarlet trees and for Kylie at last these, too, had beauty. She looked up the mountain towards the mine, thinking of the women, the babies, flies crawling into their eyes, the pathetic skinny limbs of the children, and thought, one must be practical. One lives in a material world—of people and work and striving, but there is also love.

And that love was Steve.